the runner

the runner

A novel by
RICHARD WATSON

Copple House Books
Lakemont, Georgia

The Runner. Copyright © 1981 by Richard A, Watson. All rights reserved. Printed in the United States of America. No part of this book may be used or reproduced in any manner whatsoever without written permission except in the case of brief quotations embodied in critical articles and reviews. For information address Copple House Books, Road's End, Lakemont, Georgia 30552.

First Edition

Library of Congress Cataloging in Publication Data

Watson, Richard A., 1931-
   The Runner

   I. Title.
PS3573.A8576R8   813'.54   80-28438
ISBN 0-932298-24-9

1

He was not fat, but he weighed thirty pounds more than he did when he had attained full growth at the age of fifteen. When he was twenty-five, his weight started creeping up, and now, at forty, he weighed 170 pounds. He was not fat. Neither was he depressed. But only that spring he had read an article in an airlines magazine about activities that were said to mitigate depression. He had read it idly, leafing through magazines, as one does who flies infrequently, unable to concentrate on the serious paper-work brought along in a briefcase. The plane landed safely. He went to his meeting, then returned home by another airline, other magazines.

The next day on the way to the office, stopped at a stoplight, he saw a jogger coming up the street, someone who was fat, someone in new running shoes, new warmup suit, someone with unattainable dreams. Gregory's scornful eyes followed the poor man until the driver in the car behind let out an irate blast on his horn. Gregory drove on.

At noon, as usual, he took his lunch—two sandwiches of white bread, butter, Miracle Whip, lettuce, and baloney, some carrot sticks, a small package of potato chips, an orange, and a childhood holdover, a Twinkie—and walked a block to the edge of a small park. Seated on a bench with a sandwich in his hand, he noticed two men he had seen many times before. From a neighboring office building, they spent the noon hour in shorts running around the small park. They did not jog. They ran. As Gregory watched, the beginning words of a paragraph in the airlines magazine article on depression came into his mind. "Long distance running ..." Long distance running, what? There had been an illustration, a photograph of a lean man and a shapely woman running across what looked like a golf course. Obviously neither one had ever been depressed, and the woman was a model. The man, however, looked authentic. He was running easily with a smile on his face in the photograph.

Gregory bit into the Twinkie behind his hand as the two men came around again. The airlines magazine picture was vivid in his mind, and as he really looked at the two runners here in the park for the first time, the background behind them faded and they took on the etched reality of the photograph. They passed without glancing down at him. Gregory closed his mouth and looked at the half-eaten Twinkie. The runners were office workers, like himself. Long distance runners.

That night he was about to get into bed when he turned instead to go back into the bathroom. There he pulled up his pajama top to look at his middle.

"What are you doing?" his wife asked.

"Nothing," Gregory said, switching off the light. He got into bed. Elizabeth snuggled comfortably against his back, and they soon fell asleep.

Next morning after his shower, he tried to look at himself in the fogged-over full-length mirror. He mopped it with his towel, but the view was not satisfactory. After a moment he reached down to scoot the bathroom scales out from the corner behind the toilet bowl. He took an involuntary deep breath as he stepped onto the scales. The mechanism racketed back and forth. When it stopped he learned that he weighed 171, call it 170, pounds.

It had been months since he had last weighed himself. And

months before that. He had thought each time over the years that he was probably as heavy as he ought to get. But he was not all that heavy. Even at 170 pounds, a man five feet eight inches tall was not really too heavy.

Gregory dressed, snugging his belt securely around his middle. He had no pot. Much of his weight was not in front, but rested just above his belt on either side, circling halfway around his back. He had large thighs and his face was full, but he looked trim in his suit. Especially in comparison to most men his age.

He had slept well and he felt good as he shook Post's 40% Bran Flakes into a bowl. He preferred Wheaties, but had switched when the twins learned to read. Donald and Constance were now fifteen.

Gregory spooned sugar on his breakfast food and into his coffee. He poured homogenized milk into the coffee and onto the breakfast food, stirred the coffee, licked the spoon, and took a bite of breakfast food. Post 40% Bran Flakes had been "improved" since he first started eating them. Before, they were smooth and uniformly colored. Now they were crinkly with flecks of lighter colored material in them. He had not noticed when the "improvement" took place, but when he discovered the change, he took up the box and read the list of ingredients. There was now no way to check whether or not the ingredients had been changed. He did think the taste was not the same—not as good—but there was no way to test that now, either.

"Penny . . ." Elizabeth said.

Gregory glanced across the table at the middle-aged woman sitting there. He had not noticed when that had happened, either. The change had surely been gradual, but he remembered distinctly the morning he had seen, across the table, not the young Elizabeth, but a middle-aged woman, talking while she buttered her toast. Elizabeth never wore a housecoat. At home she wore jeans and his cast-off dress shirts, neatly tucked in. It was still Elizabeth. She was heavier, of course, than when he had married her. Her skin and breasts sagged now. But what had struck him most, that morning as she bit into her toast, was the conviction that her teeth were now crooked as they had not been before. This he could check. When Gregory looked at the old photographs he discovered that Elizabeth's teeth had always been crooked.

"Oh, nothing ... the twins ...?" Gregory tipped his head toward the back door.

"Oh, they were up and gone hours ago," Elizabeth said. "Something at school."

Gregory had turned to the morning paper beside his bowl. Elizabeth sat with one leg up in her chair, the other crossed over it. She swung her free foot and ate her toast. Gregory was vaguely aware that she had already eaten breakfast with the twins—she made them eat breakfast—and was eating to keep him company now. They did not speak again until he had his briefcase and sack lunch in hand, and was at the door.

"Bye-bye, have a good day," Elizabeth said, pecking him on the cheek.

"Good-by."

Gregory had gone to college with the specific intent of becoming a Certified Public Accountant. He had been good in mathematics in high school, and when he was drafted, he had been placed in the army accounting branch. He had not minded it. Moreover, the Captain in charge had liked him, and had told him many times that a good CPA is never out of work. Gregory could have earned his certificate at a business school in two years, but he had the Korean Bill of Rights—although he had not gone to Korea—so he went up to the state university in Minneapolis where he took the full four years, majoring with a B.A. in Accounting.

He had met Elizabeth the first semester in a required English class. Elizabeth was from St. Paul, and she was easily amused by Gregory's stories about Northwood and what she insisted were his small town ways. Both were satisfied, so they were married in June at the end of their sophomore year. Elizabeth's parents were impressed with Gregory's maturity, and they readily agreed to continue to support Elizabeth so she could finish her schooling, too. She got a secondary school teacher's certificate at graduation, and taught Social Studies one year in the Minneapolis school system before the twins came. Gregory had been high in his class and had been offered a good job in a down-town firm. He was pleased—both of them liked Minneapolis—and at once he took out an FHA loan on a house overlooking a small lake in the western suburbs. It was only a fifteen minute drive to the office.

Gregory had worked now for sixteen years, and was head of his division. He had been promised that he would soon be made a vice-president. His work would be much the same, but he would shift to sharing profits. More money. He did not need it. The loan on the house would be paid off in four years. That would mean more money for other things each month. It would mean more spending money for the twins no doubt, when they were in college. Despite rising tuition costs, there would be no problem there. As soon as Gregory had learned that Elizabeth might be carrying twins, he had looked carefully into several plans. When they were born, he started investing in their names, and now had ample funds to cover their four years. Elizabeth wanted Donald to go on to law school, to rise above his father's station. Fine. There would be enough for that, too.

Gregory sat on the park bench, eating his lunch, watching the runners go by.

2

Some weeks later, Gregory, Elizabeth, and the twins went to the Northwest Plaza for a shopping tour. They did this frequently, with few plans, and all enjoyed it. On such occasions they would fill three grocery carts at the A&P, and inevitably someone would buy some item of clothing that had to be returned. Gregory remembered the large family gatherings of his childhood in Northwood. Both of his parents had grown up there, had brothers and sisters living close, and every Sunday some of them had gotten together. Gregory's sister had married in Northwood and had no children. As for Elizabeth, she was an only child. And her parents had not demanded attention. Gregory's family had eaten with them once a month until two years ago when Elizabeth's father had retired, sold his house, and moved to Florida. There was no extended family. Instead, the shopping sprees, from the excitement of the twins when they were infants to the veneer of their present blasé teen-aged sophistication, cemented his family's togetherness, their greatest pleasure, their time of open family feeling for one another. They trooped into all the stores together, Gregory flourished the Master Charge, they ate in the Pizza Hut, topped it off with ice cream at Baskin-Robbins, and went home tired but seldom really crabby. It was after such a day, after dozing off with popcorn and beer in front of television, that Gregory and

Elizabeth would go to bed and make love. They would hold one another, talk of the twins, of the day, of something in the past, something on television.

They had gone on few vacations. The lake was right out the front door for fishing and swimming and sailing, and Gregory liked to work around the house. Over the years he had paneled rooms with pine, built in cabinets, book cases, window seats. Elizabeth worked on the yard and landscaping, kept a garden, and painted the woodwork. Property values had appreciated and there was inflation, but Gregory and Elizabeth knew that the threefold increase in value of their property over its purchase price was partly a result of their own work. They talked of this. And they toyed with the notion of a real vacation when the twins were in college. They would take a Windjammer Cruise in the Caribbean. That would be something, after twenty years of sailing Sunfish and Penguins on the lake.

The twins wanted to go to JEANS WEST, so they all set off toward it across the plaza. The last time they had been here the store next door had been vacant, but now it was THE ATHLETE'S FOOT, with windows full of striped and garishly colored running shoes.

"Wow! Look at those," Donald said, but he rushed on past into JEANS WEST. Constance was close behind.

Gregory paused. "I think," he said, "I think I'll just look in here a minute."

Elizabeth nodded briskly. These were school clothes the twins were buying—it was August—and although Elizabeth had largely lost control of what they wore, she was still intent on supervising. She followed the twins.

Gregory pushed open the door of THE ATHLETE'S FOOT and went inside. The displays were blazes of bright color. Seemingly hundreds of multi-colored shoes, toes down, were displayed flat against the back wall. Round racks of T-shirts, polo shirts, tank top shirts, and sweat shirts, rows of running shorts in cotton and nylon, wire manikins wearing warmup suits, all in solid, demanding colors of chemical brightness. Even the white socks, a hundred dozen pairs on prongs, had stripes at their tops of Kelly Green, Prussian Blue, Pumpkin Orange. Everything was neat, the shop was clean, and after a moment, Gregory absorbed the wash of color. There was nothing in the shop that did not have functionally to do with running.

No one bothered Gregory as he walked around. Two boys were trying on shoes, their parents and evidently a sister—another family group—hovering about. Two young clerks were helping them, a boy and a girl. Half a dozen other young people were looking at the clothes on the racks. They were quiet, obviously well-behaved. Gregory observed that several of them wore running shoes.

The girl was putting shoes in boxes, the two boys must have tried on a dozen pairs each.

"Can I help?" she smiled up at Gregory.

He hesitated, but then sat down in the chair.

"I was thinking ... of running shoes."

"Did you have any in mind?"

Gregory was looking at the wall of shoes.

"I wore Converse All-Stars in high school," he said, the old brand name popping in to his head. He laughed nervously, but the girl's laughter was so spontaneous and uninhibited that he lost his nervousness.

"Well, I played basketball in high school, you know." He had not really been tall enough, but as a guard he could set up plays for the fast-breaking style of the 1950s. He would not make the team now, he thought. Last year the Northwood team had gone to the state tournament, and every player on the squad was over six feet tall. They had a center who was six-ten. Where did they come from?

"Have you been running?"

"No, well some." He had been on the baseball team, too.

Shortstop. He was good. But Northwood was a small town. They did not have track, only baseball and basketball. Would those Minnesota farmers have understood anything else? Football, maybe, but the high school was too small for that then. Gregory thought, though, that maybe Northwood did have a track team now. They had football.

The girl had taken his size, and now was back with an armload of shoe boxes. Gregory took off both his shoes and pulled on thick socks from a basket as the clerk instructed.

"The sizes are all different," she said. "We'll try an 8 Nike Cortez, but if you wear an 8D street shoe, it may be too narrow."

It was, as was the 8½ he tried next.

"Well, let's try these," she said. "These are New Balance's 320. They were first in *Runner's World* survey," she glanced up, and went on when she saw that *Runner's World* had drawn a blank. "You know, they rank all the shoes every year. New Balance comes in widths, most of them don't. I've brought an 8½E here for you."

Gregory stood up in the shoe.

"It feels a little tight across the ball of the foot."

"Yes," she felt his foot," and we can't loosen it because it doesn't lace all the way down. And we don't have a double-E, only a D besides the E. Well, let's try this one, this is a Brooks Villanova. It was number two, and is the best bargain of any shoe in the place, only $20."

It seemed to fit all right. Gregory put the other shoe on and stood up.

"Jog around," the girl indicated. "See how they feel."

She had waved vaguely and now Gregory saw that the displays and counter were designed so that there was room to run all the way around the shop. He trotted self-consciously around.

"They seem to slip at the heel."

The girl jammed her finger down the back of the shoe.

"Yep."

Size 8 was too tight.

"Well, let's try this one, this is a Puma. Made in Germany. Not everyone likes the brand, and it's not in the top ten, but it's the one we usually try on people with wide feet."

It fit fine, but was too long.

"Heck," the girl said. "Well," she went on, "you could go across the plaza to THE SHOE WORKS. They stock Puma and might have an 8."

Gregory looked over at the young man who seemed to be the manager. He was leaning on the counter watching them, but he had not reacted at all when the girl suggested that Gregory go to a competitor.

"I'm sorry . . ." Gregory began.

The girl laughed again. "Think nothing of it. I've tried on every shoe in the place myself."

Gregory did not get up.

The girl paused, and then said, "How would you like to try on the best shoes in the house?"

Gregory nodded assent.

"Most expensive, too," the girl smiled over her shoulder.

She was back almost at once.

"Ok, these are Adidas SL. They were high last year, but only number eleven this. Still one of the best shoes, and we have both last year's and this year's models."

Gregory put on the shoe, then untied it to loosen the laces.

"Yes, it's better laced all the way down like that," she said.

Gregory trotted around the shop without thinking of being self-conscious this time. They did not feel bad, but the arch support seemed to press in too much.

"They do fit," he said, but the girl was unboxing another pair.

"These are the end-all," she said, "best and most expensive, Nike LD1000, $40."

Gregory gawked at the shoes as she slipped one on him. He picked up the other shoe. His sense of color had returned. These were deep yellow nylon mesh with the Nike slash on the sides in fluorescent orange. The suede leather toe and heel coverings were greenish, the laces brilliant white. The body of the shoe was seated on a wedge of white rubber that flared down to a black bottom sole, turned up at the toe and very wide and square at the back. The sole was covered with quarter-inch square protrusions. The sole said U.S. Patent No. 3793750.

"They patented these soles," the clerk said, as she took the shoe and put in on his other foot.

Gregory stood up and looked down. These were moon-walking shoes. He trotted around the room. No shoes he had ever tried on fit better. His feet felt good in them. When had he last felt his feet?

He could tell by the way the girl was smiling that she knew. She did know. He had seldom had a clerk who knew her product so well. It would have been foolish to ask her if she were a runner. He knew by now that the three stripes on her shoes meant that she was wearing Adidas, but not, he thought, the SL model he had tried on. She was trim and thin in Levi's and T-shirt.

"You'll need socks," she said. "How about blue tops?" She pulled two pair down. "Now some people don't, but I think you ought to wear these thin cotton liner socks under the thick ones. They take up sweat, and there's some nylon in the thicker socks, and as they wear out those nylon threads can cut your feet." She had put two pair of the cotton socks with the others. "Anything else?"

Gregory looked toward the racks of clothes.

"Try them on," the girl said, beginning to match shoes to put in the boxes piled on the floor. "There's a dressing room over there."

Well, perhaps he had better try on the shorts. He had not worn any of this type since high school. He found a pair of white medium, 32-34. His belt size was 34.

They were too small. They went around his middle, but he could not bend over. Made for boys? He had noticed before in buying jeans that some of them supposedly his size were so tight that he could not get his legs into them. He put his pants back on, went out and brought back a pair of large shorts, 36-38, also white. They fit.

"I wonder," Gregory said, fingering the motif embossed on the shorts, "do you have any plain ones?" It was a running foot with wings and the words: THE ATHLETE'S FOOT.

"No, I'm sorry, they all have that."

"All right," Gregory said.

"How about a T-shirt?"

Gregory had plenty of T-shirts, but he laughed and said, "Ok, why not? I wouldn't want to be conspicuous." He went over to the rack and picked out a bright orange shirt that said across its front, simply, in blue letters: NIKE.

The bill was nearly $60. Gregory gave the girl his Master Charge.

"Thank you very much," she said.

"Thank you so much," Gregory replied, self-conscious again as he walked out the door dangling the plastic bag from his hand, a white bag with a large THE ATHLETE'S FOOT design, out into the dull colors.

He did not know how long he had been in THE ATHLETE'S FOOT, but evidently quite a while, for when he came up to them in JEANS WEST, Elizabeth said, "You're just in time. Where's the Master Charge?"

"Whatcha got?" Donald asked, poking the plastic bag.

"You'll see soon enough," Gregory said, worrying.

He put the bag between his knees while he signed the charge form.

"What is it?" Constance asked, adding, "you were gone a long time. I'll show you what I got if you show me what you got."

Donald guffawed, and Elizabeth frowned at him.

Gregory sighed. "All right," he said. "Let's all get a Dairy Queen and we can sit on the bench out in front and look at what we've got."

13

As always, Gregory ordered a large strawberry sundae.

Donald pulled the shoe box out of the bag, but allowed Constance to take it to open.

None of them said a word when the shoes were exposed. Donald looked from the shoes up at his father and finally whistled slowly.

"Zowie, dad, I mean, *what* a pair of shoes!"

Constance had taken out the shorts and the T-shirt.

"Hey, mom," she said, "you ought to take up jogging, too."

Gregory lifted his head quickly to look, blank faced, at Elizabeth.

"Huh," she said, "not me. Can you see a plump chicken like me running around the lake in one of those suits?" She puffed out her cheeks and held out her elbows, flapping them up and down.

Gregory relaxed and laughed with the others as he took the shoes and put them carefully back into the box.

"Let's take all this junk to the car and then continue," he said. "I want to go to the hardware store."

They stuffed the Dairy Queen cups and spoons into the disposal can and then carried the packages to the car. Gregory had not looked at Constance's purchases.

They got home about seven in the evening. The late summer sun was still high. After everything had been put away, Gregory sat at the kitchen table, watching television. Even after the pizza and ice cream, he always felt that they ought to have dinner when they got home. Elizabeth sat down at the table.

"Nothing on TV," Gregory said. He looked up to find Elizabeth staring at him. Then she grinned.

"Go on. It'll be light another hour. Try them out."

Gregory blushed, and Elizabeth, seeing it, laughed out loud.

"Go on now, that's what you got them for."

"All right," Gregory said, getting up.

"They *are* a little loud," Elizabeth said.

Gregory hurried upstairs to change, his thoughts already

bounding. He walked through the front room, where the twins were watching television on the color set. Donald said, "Oo-la-la," and Constance whistled.

Gregory stepped out the front door. It had not been so bad as he had feared. They were just teasing him. Gregory, like many fairly close men of his generation, of his Middle Western upbringing, of his profession, of his time of life, of his limited experience, was sentimental about his family. He blinked back tears as he walked hurriedly down to the lakeshore.

There was a trail all the way around the lake, just two miles someone had once measured. When Gregory and Elizabeth had first moved to their house, they had walked all the way around. He did not think he had been all the way around on foot again since. Well, two miles was not that far.

He had started out too fast. After 100 yards, Gregory was shocked to realize that he was going to have to stop. He was gasping for breath, his chest was full of shooting pains, and he had a stitch in his side. He slowed to a walk, kept on walking. When he caught his breath he thought wryly that his feet still felt fine. After a few minutes he started jogging very slowly, and got about half a mile before he had to walk again. Walking and jogging, he made his way around the lake.

He could see that Elizabeth and the twins were waiting for him. Long before he should have, he started his final run for home. Again he was going too fast, but he forced himself to continue up the grassy slope from the lake, to the front door, to their cheers. Elizabeth looked concerned, but he nodded through his gasps that he was all right. The twins went right back to the television. Elizabeth had probably made them come out.

"Go take a shower," Elizabeth squeezed his hand. "I'll make a big bowl of popcorn."

Gregory's knees were weak as he walked up the stairs, but by the time he had showered he was feeling better. He and Elizabeth sat talking at the kitchen table with the popcorn and beer. Usually at this time of day Gregory was dozing in his chair in front of television. Now he was wide awake. He talked again of the Windjammer Cruise, drawing Elizabeth into his excitement.

They were still full of the novelty of the day when they made love that night. Elizabeth slipped off to sleep immediately, but Gregory lay awake, thinking of his run, worried about how out of shape he was.

Next morning Elizabeth threatened to drag him from the bed. Then she let him lie. It was Sunday, after all. When he got up he could not wake up. He shaved sloppily. The shower helped some, but every muscle in his body was sore. When he walked down the stairs, his back hurt, and there seemed to be thumb tacks under his knee caps. He ate his breakfast dejectedly, and spent a long time reading the paper. He was too stiff to work around the house, and although he thought about it, he did not try to run that day. When Elizabeth asked him how he felt as they were going to bed, he groaned. It was a lost day. Gregory had trouble getting to sleep, but on Monday he awoke early, still aching.

At noon, he took his lunch to the park as usual, at first ignoring the runners. Then he found himself observing them closely. They really could run. He wondered how fast. Estimating the distance, he timed one of their swings around the park. It would be about seven or seven and a half minutes a mile. Gregory was disappointed. That did not seem to be very fast.

When Gregory got home that evening he changed immediately into his running clothes. Elizabeth frowned when he asked her to plan dinner slightly later than usual.

Gregory checked his watch, then doggedly pushed halfway around the lake without stopping to walk. He looked at his watch and was astonished to see that it had taken him twelve minutes and twenty-five seconds, well, say, twelve minutes. Twelve minutes a mile! Gregory walked a few minutes to catch his breath, then jogged the rest of the way around the lake. He was still annoyed when he came down from his shower, and he snapped at the twins at dinner. However, he did feel better than he had after the first time. And he seemed to be too awake to watch television so he compromised by reading a mystery novel instead. He enjoyed reading, but had not done much for years.

The next evening he left his watch at home. After five days of jogging, the stiffness in his muscles started to recede. After a week, he jogged all the way around the lake without stopping. By cold weather he was going around twice. He had returned to THE ATHLETE'S FOOT to buy a Navy Blue warmup suit (with red and white stripes down the arms and legs), and duofold long underwear the girl had suggested for the cold weather ahead. Mud and weather had blunted the color of his shoes, but the orange Nike slash would always stand out. By the time the weather got really cold, Gregory was thinking of going around three times, six miles. But he decided to wait until spring. He had eventually taken his watch again, to find that he could run four miles in about thirty-six minutes, nine minutes a mile. That still seemed slow. What he could do the rest of the winter was see if he could get it down to eight minutes a mile.

3

It had not been easy at the beginning. That first time Gregory had run around the lake had nearly been the last. His bones were jammed, his knees bent wrong, his head snapped on his neck. He could not breathe and his legs felt like lead. After his final effort to reach the door where Elizabeth and the twins were waiting, he felt that he had inadvertently made a turn just to the side of his usual ways to find himself in a chamber of horror. The cheering and cheerfulness of his family seemed a veneer on underlying mockery. What did they know? Or, rather, did they not know? And were they not really baiting him, scorning him for his folly? But no. Their show of family fun was not a mask. That was what they were. They simply did not know what he was feeling, what he had undergone.

Later, lying in the tub of hot water recovering, too weak in the knees to stand for a shower, he marveled at this other world that had lain all these years just outside his front door without his knowing it. Without his realizing it, he was incapable of doing a simple thing like running two miles. He had thought of himself as healthy, which in a manner of speaking he was—he was seldom sick—but also he had thought of himself as fit, which he was not. He had thought that he could buy some shoes and get a little exercise, run around the lake as those two men ran around the park. But now he wondered, seriously doubted.

He had turned just slightly off the beaten track to find, not just an acceleration of a brisk walk around the block, but another dimension of locomotion. You do not just go smoothly from walking to running, as he had evidently assumed. It turned out to be a steep step, a hard jolt. Gregory was stunned. He ate popcorn automatically, wiping butter from his hands with the kitchen towel. He drank the beer that strangely did not quench his thirst, and by the time he went to bed that night, he was ready to face the truth. He had been frightened. As he had gasped for breath at the door, waving off Elizabeth's concern, trying to make a wisecrack at the twins' perfunctory cheering, he had been scared to death.

Lying on his back in bed with his hands behind his head, his thinking position (when he was ready to go to sleep he rolled over on his stomach), Gregory felt relatively safe again. If he were ever going to have a heart attack, it would probably have been then, and he had read enough to be pretty sure that he had not had even a mild attack. But he probably had not done himself any good, either.

Well, that fright he could put behind him. But there was a colder fear of what was ahead, one that caused a chill to course his spine several times before he rolled over to sleep.

Could he really do it? He just did not know. It seemed so easy. So many people were jogging these days. Those two in the park, they talked and laughed as they ran. But he could not even run two miles. It was not just that he was out of shape. His whole body had felt wrong. His body had protested strongly, and at the end he had had to fight it with every ounce of will power at his command. Whose body was it? He was not even sure that he had won.

Gregory had thought he would take up running. It was not that easy. That pleasant-looking bright-colored world was protected by barriers of difficulty and pain he had not anticipated. He would have to fight his way through. It was not just that he feared a repetition of that awful trip around the lake, or the possibility of even worse struggles ahead. He was afraid that he had gotten into something that he did not even like. Why had he decided to take up running in the first place?

Gregory rolled over, sighed, and went to sleep.

He brooded the next day, and on that third day, he tried again. It was painful—he was very stiff—but it was not so bad. For one thing, he did not sprint to the door at the end. Neither were Elizabeth and the twins waiting for him. It was a struggle, but he did gain the confidence that he could push himself around.

And then day after day, it got easier. He passed through the barrier. His body resigned itself to the new regime. His breathing got easier before his muscles adjusted. He was glad he had stopped smoking half a dozen years ago when the big cancer campaigns had begun. Elizabeth had quit then, too, but she started again after a few months. This had annoyed Gregory at the time, but he stuck it out and the only thing that bothered him about Elizabeth's smoking now was the irritation of the smoke. He had lost all desire for cigarettes himself. And he soon breathed easily as he ran around the lake.

He had not been in such bad shape after all. He ran every day for a month, until he could go around the lake without difficulty. But it had become a bore. Gregory slacked off, finding excuses for not running in work around the house, forgetting, just deciding not to. He soon saw the pattern. If he did not run for three days, his muscles got sore when he started again. Then in mid-summer they went to Florida on vacation to visit Elizabeth's parents, and Gregory did not run for two weeks. The first time he ran after that was not quite like the first time, for his wind was ok, but his muscles had reverted and they protested with much stiffness the next day.

Well, one took up running or one did not. Gregory accepted the boredom, and from then on rarely missed a day. And one day he simply continued running after circling the lake once, and went right on around a second time. Four miles. He felt fine, and ran four miles after that. He quit thinking about why. He was obviously fitter now than he had been since high school, and that was good enough reason. He did not want to be one of those men who got overheated and out of breath when he had to walk up a few flights of stairs.

The need for his daily run crept up on Gregory. He had had to make it a focal point of the day because if he did not do it immediately on returning home from the office, he would not do it. It was more important in his day, then, than it really was. He chided himself about this, and tried to explain in a harrassed way to a slightly amused and slightly annoyed Elizabeth.

"You just go ahead and have your run," she said, patting him on the cheek.

Gregory had never told her about the fear.

It was late fall when he noticed that all remnants of dread and distaste had gone, and that, in the office, he was looking forward to the end of the day when he could have his run. As the leaves had turned color and the weather cooled, Gregory began to experience the pleasure of runnning. It was not just for now, not for the deep reds of the maples and the yellows of the willows, the scudding wind across the blue-green lake, the dark migrating geese, the billowing white clouds, the browning grass. It was also the thought of running again when this day was gone. And then the past was recreated. Gregory now chuckled with pleasure at the thought of that first time around the lake. He gloried in remembrance of his aches and pains. He indulged in pride at his determination, at the backbone that had kept him going through those tough early days. He had decided to be a runner. And he was.

4

It was the best winter of Gregory's life. Probably it was for Elizabeth, too. Gregory knew that when a man reached forty he was supposed to go into the doldrums, lose interest in his job and in sex, or start chasing young women. But none of this happened to Gregory. As he sat back savoring a second huge piece of chocolate cake—as he preferred—washing it down with glasses of whole milk on his forty-first birthday, he felt a wave of sentimental nostalgia. It had been a good life, Elizabeth was great, the twins were great. He concealed involuntary tears by blowing his nose.

As for sex, Gregory's interest and appetite had increased. In their early thirties, he and Elizabeth had drifted into a weekend pattern. Saturday night and Sunday morning, and not always on Sunday. Twice a week at most. But all that winter they had made love at least five times a week, often in the mornings. Gregory did not need to be at work before nine, and once again he blessed his foresight in buying a house only a short drive from the office. He was waking up earlier in the morning since he started running, and he was feeling better. Elizabeth would have the twins off to school by seven-thirty, plenty of time for her to return to bed for half an hour. Gregory would wake up at seven, doze on his back hearing the rush of the twins' breakfast and leave-taking, the slam of the door, and by the time Elizabeth padded back through the quiet house to the bedroom, he would be erect, excited, anticipating. It was always good. Sometimes it was spectacular for them both.

Afterward, by eight or eight-fifteen at the latest, Gregory would be in the shower, his body singing (but not out loud). He ate a hearty breakfast, having added fried eggs and bacon to his coffee and Post's 40% Bran Flakes. He had also recently started slicing a banana on his cereal. He left the house at eight-forty, plenty of time to reach the office. And when he got there, the work went well. Also, the time seemed to pass more rapidly, now that he had his run to look forward to. The end of the day did not come at five now, but rather after his run around the lake. Elizabeth had changed dinner from six to seven, making Gregory's running and evening shower schedule very calm and leisurely. The twins had complained for a day or two, but had adjusted quickly. This orderly life sat well with Gregory.

The long underwear was necessary. It sometimes stayed below zero for weeks in Minneapolis. Gregory wore gloves, and often he wore a skier's face mask. The sharp air sometimes penetrated his lungs, needles of ice, but he was breathing so easily as he ran now that he could take shallow breaths on the coldest days.

He almost never missed a day, even when it was raining and snowing, even the weeks of wind and drifts. The lake froze. Gregory circled it.

The only trouble was that his speed did not increase. Once on a perfect day in mid-winter he had made the double circuit in just over thirty-two minutes, eight minutes a mile. But thereafter his best times were eight and a half, and as late winter settled in he more often ran nine, and in the snow, ten minutes a mile. Wait until spring.

During the winter Gregory ate his lunch at the office. However, it was still an old-fashioned firm that closed down for the full noon hour, and although Gregory often worked straight through, eating at his desk, there was plenty of time, so if the day was fine or he was restless, he often took a walk. Usually he would stroll around the park. He had a sense of fellow feeling for the two runners, so that he always shivered to see them running in shorts even in the bitterest weather. Sometimes he timed them, and figured that their speed was down to six minutes a mile. Now he decided that that was fairly fast.

It was cold, but the sun was creeping back to the north, each day staying longer in the western sky. The lake was still frozen over, and as Gregory ran, the red sun would settle, pause, flatten a little—but not enlarge, that was for summer—and sink far off there beneath the horizon. Gregory had been raised with the seasons, spring and fall baseball, winter basketball, summer for fishing and swimming and working on one of his uncles' farms. And life here, despite being in the heart of suburbia, was clocked by the lake's seasons. There were baby ducks in the spring, sailing and fishing in summer, fall hauling out of boats, winter skating. But in seventeen years by the lake, this was the first that Gregory had observed it close at hand, out in the weather, day by day. And as the days lengthened, he could feel—with the lake—the coming of spring. He was exhilarated as he could not remember being for years.

One particularly fine day in late winter the sun's last rays shot horizontally through low clouds laying pink and green stripes across the sky and on the rotting ice. Gregory's heart leapt up and in a surge of strength he started to sprint—a real run—the last hundred yards from the lake path up the slope to the door. There was a tearing pain in his right calf. Gregory stopped instantly. The pain passed, but when he put his foot down, it was there again. Gregory slowly limped the rest of the way home, stepping only on the toe of his right foot. Thank goodness it had not happened half way around the lake.

"Charley horse," he told Elizabeth. "I haven't had one since high school." He felt drained, sitting on a kitchen chair in his long underwear. "I wonder how long it takes to heal up?" he asked peevishly.

"Heat pad, maybe?" Elizabeth asked. She almost seemed frightened, and had said very little.

"No, I'll take a hot bath." Gregory continued sitting. Then he struggled to his feet, relenting. "Maybe later, probably be the best thing." He went slowly and carefully up the stairs. After the long soak his calf did feel better. But when he pressed in with his thumbs there was a deep and insistent pain. He would not be running for awhile.

The charley horse was a firm presence the next morning. Gregory could feel the pain when he drove the car. At the office he tried to walk normally, but he could not conceal his limp. Several people commiserated with him. Someone suggested that he had slipped on the ice, and he let that stand. He had told no one that he was running. So far as he knew, no one knew but Elizabeth and the twins, and a few neighbors living around the lake.

That day at the office Gregory did not move around much, but the next at noon—with his leg not any better—Gregory walked carefully out to the elevator and went down to the street. He crossed slowly and made his way over to the park.

The two runners were there as usual. Gregory had never waved or nodded at them, nor they at him, although he supposed that they were vaguely aware of his regular presence as he once had been of theirs. He could not stop them. But he knew their building, so made his way to its door. He would be late getting back to the office, but he could blame it on his leg. He did not want to set a bad example.

The runners did not give themselves much time to get back to work. Gregory wondered what they did about a shower. It was five to one before they pulled up to a stop where Gregory was waiting. They would have walked right on by.

"Excuse me, but . . ." Gregory began.

One of them pushed on in the door, but the other stopped. "Yeah?"

"I wanted to ask . . ."

"Let's go on in," the runner said, "cold out here."

Gregory followed him in the door, and then, uncomfortably, on into a janitor's locker room. It had a shower. The runners undressed, stepped under the shower briefly, then rubbed themselves down with towels.

"Yeah?" the one said again to Gregory, unlocking a locker on the wall and beginning to dress rapidly.

"I have," Gregory began. "Well, look," he pulled up his pantleg. There was not much to see, but he pressed his thumbs into his calf, wincing slightly.

"Been running? Say, my name's Fred. This here's Gene."

Gregory reached up and shook hands. "Gregory."

"Charley horse, eh?" Fred said.

Gregory finally opened up. "I've been running since last spring, almost a year. Four miles a day, not very fast, not like you guys, only eight minutes a mile, eight and half. And I haven't had any trouble at all, but a couple of days ago this happened."

"Do any warmups?" Fred asked.

Gene was already dressed. "See you tomorrow," he said, leaving. He had shaken Gregory's hand, but had paid no other attention to him.

"Exercises, you mean? No."

"Awfully cold to run in this weather. Gotta warm those old muscles up."

"But you guys run in shorts. I run in long underwear and a warmup suit."

Fred grinned, and his glance at Gregory's middle was as though he had poked him with a finger. Gregory had noticed before, of course, that these two runners were thin, but without their clothes they had looked almost emaciated. Except for those long stringy muscles, one might think them weak. Fred had dressed by this time, but unlike Gene he seemed relaxed, and gave no indication that he wanted to rush off.

Fred said nothing more, and after an awkward silence, what he had said soaked in.

"You mean," Gregory said slowly, "as you get older you can't take it as much."

Gregory had not considered how old Fred and Gene were. He still thought of himself as a young man, and he joked that he had trouble telling just how old people were once they got into their twenties. Now he put aside that conceit and estimated that Fred and Gene were twenty-five, at most twenty-six. They must think him ancient. That's what he thought about anyone over forty when he was their age.

Fred had caught the tone, and he looked concerned.

"Yes, that's true," he said seriously. "But that's no reason for anyone's not running. I know several runners in their forties. Ted Corbet is over fifty and still a top double Marathoner. People run in their sixties and seventies. It's all a matter of preparing, of doing it the right way."

Fred nodded, an empty vessel.

"Do you do any exercises at all?" Fred asked again.

"No."

"Well, look," Fred said, glancing at his watch. He seemed suddenly bored with it all. "Warm up for ten minutes before you run from now on."

"But what about now?" Gregory said, hobbling out of the locker room after Fred.

"Oh," Fred stopped. He forgot his hurry. "Here," he said, pushing out the door of the building, "stand about this far from the wall."

Gregory stood beside Fred.

Now Fred leaned over to put his palms against the wall.

"Keep your legs and body straight. Lock your knees, make your knee caps go up, tight. Ok, now keep your feet flat on the floor, ground, sidewalk, where are we, anyway?"

Gregory laughed nervously with him. They were on the sidewalk and people were looking.

Fred was oblivious. "Try it. Ok, back up now, keeping your feet together and flat on the sidewalk. Bend over as far as you can. You feel it, don't you? This is the way to stretch that calf muscle. You see, they tighten up. They shorten when you run. You want to stretch them out again. Do this three or four times a day, and always before you run."

Fred had straightened up.

"How long will it take to heal?" Gregory asked.

"Depends. Do the stretching. But you'd better stay off it awhile. Takes longer to heal the older you are. You'll be able to tell when it's time."

Fred hit his forehead with the heel of his hand and grinned.

"What am I doing outside again? You'd think maybe I didn't want to go back to work." He opened the door to the building. "And take it easy when you start in again," Fred said as the door slowly closed. "It takes time."

"Thanks . . . Fred," Gregory said. It was nearly one-thirty by the time Gregory got back to his desk, but no one noticed.

He stretched regularly, but it was a month before he dared run again, and two weeks after that before he felt that he was out of danger of recurrence. By then spring was definitely on its way.

5

One morning in early spring after Gregory had been running for just over two years, Elizabeth brought the paper up to bed after the twins had left for school. She usually folded it beside Gregory's place at the table so he could skim through it while eating breakfast. And it was not exactly what he had in mind now.

"Look at this," Elizabeth said, folding back the paper and scoring an article with her thumbnail. She was fully dressed. She leaned over the bed to her night table to shake a cigarette from a package there, and sat cross-legged beside Gregory on the bed, arms akimbo, blowing smoke upward past a half-closed eye, away from Gregory. Gregory sighed and looked at the paper.

It was an article about the Annual Twin City Memorial Day Run. He had already seen a notice of it that Elizabeth had evidently missed. He read through the article and looked up quizzically, as though he did not already know.

"Well?" Elizabeth said.

"Well what?"

"Aren't you going to enter?"

Gregory's look hardened. He said nothing.

Elizabeth seemed surprised only for an instant. She skipped over annoyance to sarcasm.

"Well, we early risers thought you might want to enter." She reached for the paper, but Gregory held it back.

"You *have* been running for something, haven't you?"

"I don't want to race."

"Well, it isn't much of a race. They want everyone, run at your own speed, they say."

Gregory knew it was not a real race. He was not sure how he felt about racing. But he knew he did not want to run with a big crowd, to be organized, pushed around, and patronized.

"You'd meet other runners there," Elizabeth said. "Maybe you'd make some new friends."

Gregory remembered well the camaraderie of high school ball teams, sweet memories. But he was a kid then, and this would not be camaraderie, anyway, it would be easy familiarity and he did not want it.

"You don't seem to like our old ones much anymore."

This last was true. Gregory had tried to weasel out of several social engagements recently. He had never liked playing bridge, it was too much like work, but he went along because Elizabeth enjoyed it. He had tried to get out of a dinner party last week by saying that all they did was eat, talk, and watch television. Elizabeth had just looked at him. They had gone to the dinner. He had never actually gotten out of going anywhere, but his reluctance was obvious.

"Seven miles, three miles, and one mile," Gregory read out loud. The fee was three dollars. If you finished in your class, you were given a T-shirt that said: RUNNER: THIRD ANNUAL TWIN CITY MEMORIAL DAY RUN. There were a dozen or more categories, by sex and age. The first three finishers in each category got trophies, the next twenty certificates. Gregory would be in the men's age 40–49 category.

Elizabeth stubbed out her cigarette and got up.

"Better come and eat breakfast."

Gregory dressed and went downstairs with the paper. Elizabeth was vacuuming the front room rug. Gregory had always hated the sound of the vacuum cleaner. Elizabeth did not shut it off when he went in for her to give him an absent-minded peck on the cheek. He went out the door into the garage. He backed out.

"Are you going to enter the Twin City Run?"

Gregory smiled weakly at his next-door neighbor, nodding stupidly at the man. "I haven't really decided," Gregory said.

However, all day at the office Gregory felt the sick inevitability of it.

When he ran around the lake that evening he was passed by two gangling teen-aged boys, friends of Donald. "We decided to get ready for the race, too," one of them shouted over his shoulder back at Gregory.

How could they be running that fast when Gregory had never seen them run before? Maybe they were on the high school track team. However, their speed dropped before they were halfway around. Gregory caught and passed them just before he finished one circuit. It gave him great satisfaction as he pounded on at his steady pace to see that they were not going around twice.

"Ok, twins," Gregory announced at the dinner table. "Your father is going to enter the race."

"Not so loud," Elizabeth calmed them down. But she looked pleased.

It seemed false to Gregory. He knew his heartiness was fake. But maybe not. The twins obviously thought it fun, and Elizabeth thought he should. Maybe he did want to do it. Maybe he should meet some runners.

Gregory filled out the form for their benefit—he checked the seven mile run—then he wrote a check for three dollars and sent it in. Some days later he received a map and an instruction sheet telling him where and when to report to pick up his number. The next day on the way home from work he drove over the route.

Since it was two miles around the lake, he would have to train by running either six or eight miles. He supposed he could figure out where half a mile was, run six and half, and then retrace the half to get back home. But that did not appeal to him.

He ran around the lake four times once. However, four times around was tedious, so the next evening he decided three times—six miles—would be enough. It was not hard to move up to six miles (in truth, the eight miles had tired him), but he still could not seem to increase his speed. He could run eight minutes a mile if he worked, but all attempts to better that speed failed. If he ran seven and a half the first circuit, he was sure to have to slow down to eight and a half or even nine for the second and third. If he waited for the third circuit to turn on the steam, he just did not speed up much, even though he worked harder and seemed to be going faster.

Once he forced himself to run seven and a half, or at least under eight, for four miles. Before he finished he was beginning to feel the pains he had felt that first day he ran. Despite his gasping and his leaden legs, he continued to jog on around for the third circuit, his total time for the six miles being no better than it had ever been.

After that Gregory worried about his entry blank. There were so many runners that they were started in groups according to speed, the fastest on the front rows, with slower runners placed farther back. Gregory had checked that he was a seven-minute-a-mile runner, thinking that if he worked on it, he would be that fast by the time of the run, a month off. But as the day came closer, he knew he would never make it. He should have checked eight minutes.

The day before the run, Gregory ran eight miles, just to make sure. He was pleased to find that eight miles now went as routinely as the six he had been doing. Evidently increasing distance by two-mile intervals was not difficult. Increasing speed was still another matter.

Gregory had worked himself up into being fairly enthusiastic about the run, but his spirits dropped when he reached the vicinity of the starting point. The year before there had been nearly 500 participants. This year it looked as though there must be a thousand, and later Gregory learned that there had been 1327.

He had worn his warmup suit over his running clothes, but slipped out of it in the car when he saw that everyone else was in shorts and shirts. He had to park the car about three blocks from the gathering place. Gregory walked self-consciously toward the registration tables, noticing the kinds of shoes other runners were wearing. There were dozens of styles.

Elizabeth and the twins stood beside him in line as he moved up to get his number. There were as many people in ordinary clothes as in running outfits, everyone was talking, no one was paying any attention to anyone else, and the noise was deafening.

"Pin it on the front or back of your shirt, whichever you want," the man said, handing him a six-inch square of heavy paper with his number on it. When you finish you'll be handed a ticket. Bring it back here to exchange for your T-shirt."

Elizabeth pinned the number on the back of Gregory's shirt. Then they stood waiting.

The run was supposed to start at nine, but it was already nine-fifteen and there were still lines of runners waiting to get their numbers. Some runners were jogging around the area. Some were doing stretching exercises.

"Hadn't you better warm up, dad?" Donald asked.

It was just foolish to continue being self-conscious. Gregory found a tree and pressed against it to stretch his calves. Then he did the routine he had begun after the charley horse had healed. He touched his toes, did deep knee bends, jumped up and down swinging his arms over his head, and did half a dozen other exercises remembered from high school and the army, each fifty times, finishing with sit-ups and push-ups.

They still were not ready to start. Gregory touched his toes a few more times, but then just waited.

At nine-forty a man in a T-shirt with TWIN CITY TRACK CLUB printed on it stood on one of the registration tables and started talking through a bull horn. The crowd quieted, but Gregory still could not hear. The bull horn had no volume, but the speaker evidently did not notice this. He walked back and forth on the table, waving his free arm.

Gregory left Elizabeth—she pulled him back for a kiss—to move closer. After he caught a few words, Gregory decided that the speaker was just repeating the route instructions. There was a big map hanging from a tree beside the table. It was all obvious.

A cheer went up from the runners near the front, then all turned to go to the starting line. Half a dozen Twin City Track Club members were lining the runners up. This start was for both the three-mile and the seven-mile runs. After a mile, the three-milers would turn off, and the others would go on a longer route.

"Seven-minutes here." The Club member took Gregory firmly by the arm and placed him in line. The placing was going rapidly. Gregory turned to look around, then pushed his way back.

"I'm eight minutes," he said to the Club member there, and got placed in line again.

Before he had time to think he heard a massive voice that needed no bull horn.

"Ready now. Get set."

The gun was very loud.

Pandemonium.

There were feet and legs everywhere. Someone shoved Gregory with both hands from behind. For twenty seconds—although it seemed much longer—it was impossible not to bump people. Then the bunch of runners streamed out in a line, the leaders already far ahead. They were occupying one lane of the street, policemen on motorcycles roaring along beside, ahead, and behind, directing traffic and closing intersections as the runners progressed.

Gregory tried to stay with the runners he had been close to when he started. One fell in to match strides beside him.

"This your first time?" he asked.

Gregory shook his head. Then he nodded. What he meant was that he was too breathless to talk. The man grinned, speeded up slightly and ran on.

Gregory concentrated on doing as well as he could. But he knew he was running too fast and that if he kept it up he would be crawling at the finish. He tried to slow down without being conspicuous. He had plenty of company.

The one-mile turnoff came very soon, and three quarters of the runners turned off there to complete the three-mile course. Now Gregory had plenty of room and he began to feel better. Topping a rise he could see the front runners far ahead of him, more than a mile already. At the half-way mark he decided to increase his speed. This was not so bad as he had anticipated. He thought he was going faster than he did around the lake. The paved road jarred him more than he was used to, but he did not have to think about where he was putting his feet as he often did at the lake.

Gregory was enjoying the run.

The last mile was on a trail through the park where they had started. Gregory faltered when he saw the crowd ahead. Runners ran past a finish chute made of ropes bedecked with colored flags, on around the park, and back through the chute to the finish line. Gregory could see runners finishing, their families and friends cheering them. A lot of runners were standing about, but Gregory thought many of them must be from the three-mile race. He looked back and was glad to see a dozen runners strung out behind him.

Gregory tried to increase his pace. People shouted at him to speed up as he came off the road onto the gravel jogging trail. It was not much better than the pavement. He did not see Elizabeth or the twins.

Track Club members were posted at each turn of the trail, unnecessarily directing the runners. Gregory nodded at their encouragement, but he was getting more and more discouraged. Soon after entering the park he was passed by a runner. Then three ran by at once. With half a mile to go, Gregory could hear someone pounding up behind him, breathing hard and running heavily.

Gregory gave it all he had. He was not going to be passed again.

From there it was a blur. The number of people along the trail increased—they were too close. There was a big crowd around the finish chute, and everyone was yelling. Gregory tried to go faster the last hundred yards before the entry to the chute, but nothing came. Just before he got there, the runner behind him struggled alongside, elbowed Gregory, and entered the chute first. Gregory gasped to the finish behind him.

A Track Club member immediately grabbed Gregory and walked him out of the way. He wrote down Gregory's number on a pad and handed him a ticket. Only then did he say, "Good going, old fellow," slapped him on the back, and turned back to capture another finisher.

Then Elizabeth reached Gregory and kissed him.

"Good going, dad" Constance said, "did you hear us yelling?"

"Why didn't you elbow that guy back?" Donald said.

"I would have," Gregory said, still breathing heavily, "if I could have caught him." He giggled slightly hysterically. "Where can I sit down?"

The grass seemed to be the only place. Gregory knelt down in an open area. Donald went to where they had stashed the cooler to get the beer and Pepsis. Constance took Gregory's ticket to go collect the T-shirt. Elizabeth sat down beside him and held his hand.

"How fast?" Gregory thought. He had no way of knowing. Better than usual, anyway.

"I'd like a shower," Gregory said when he had finished the beer.

"But what about the picnic?" Elizabeth asked. She was genuinely disappointed.

Gregory looked around. "People aren't staying," he said.

And it was true. Half the crowd had left already. There were many fewer runners around now than when he had reached the park no more than twenty minutes ago. It was the most anarchistic gathering he had ever been in. A few people spoke to each other, but no one paid any attention to Gregory and his family. He had not seen a single person he knew, although Donald's two friends had been in the three-mile. Elizabeth had noticed, too, so she got up without further argument. No one was staying for a picnic.

Gregory let Elizabeth drive home. After he had his shower, they ate their picnic lunch down by the lake. By one o'clock, there was nothing to do. Gregory had been exhausted at the end of the race, but now he felt fine.

The whole afternoon stretched ahead, and Gregory had already had his run. He tried to watch the ballgame on television with Donald, but he had lately lost patience with ballgames. Finally he went out to the garage to putter. Seeing the lawn mower, he gassed it up and went out to mow the lawn. Then he continued mowing a vast section of the area he and the neighbors kept mowed on the slope down to the lake, walking along, following dumbly in the mindless noise.

He wondered how fast he had run.

He found out the next day. In tiny print, the names and times of all the runners who had finished were printed on the sports page. Gregory's time for the seven miles was 64:32. But that was more than nine minutes a mile. He could not have taken over an hour. He was sure he was going at least eight and a half minutes a mile.

The winner had done it in 34:11.

It did not make Gregory feel better that his name and time were about midway in the list, that some runners had taken twelve minutes a mile or more. They must have been walking.

The story pointed out that the winning times this year were not so good as those of the last two years. The first year only a few people competed, and most of the winners were Twin City Track Club members. Many Track Club members won last year, too, particularly in the older age groups, but they decided afterward that there were so many other runners that Club members should stay out of the race. So in this third year, Club members merely supervised.

By this time Gregory had looked in more detail. In his group—men's seven-mile, age 40–49—the winner had run just over six minutes a mile. Three minutes a mile faster than Gregory. He wondered how old the guy was.

As he put the lawn mower back in the garage at dusk, a vivid image came to Gregory. He could feel the Track Club member pulling him out of the way at the finish. He could hear what he said:

"Good going, old fellow."

Gregory went to the refrigerator for a beer. It would be a pot-luck supper as usual, on Sundays and holidays, out of the refrigerator. Later Elizabeth would pop corn. Gregory sat down at the kitchen table and pulled the tab on the beer. He took a sip and looked out the window. The bright kitchen lights made it already dark out there.

Old fellow.

6

"You did good," Elizabeth said, snuggling up to him in bed that night.

But Gregory knew she was disappointed. And puzzled. It was not what she had expected at all. At the park she had marveled at the grey-haired men who had come in much sooner than Gregory. There was really nothing she and Gregory could discuss about the race.

Gregory was up at six the next morning. He was drinking coffee, waiting for the paper to arrive, when Constance came down to breakfast. She was wearing the Memorial Day Run T-shirt.

Elizabeth looked up. "Take that off," she flashed. "That's daddy's. Connie, take it off."

Constance's happy expression faded, and she turned to go back to her room.

"No, no," Gregory spoke up, "that's all right. You can have it. It looks fine."

"But it's yours, you won it," Constance said.

"I'd never wear it, pet," Gregory said gently. "You know that," he went on, looking at Elizabeth.

Elizabeth looked resigned. She shrugged her shoulders and said, "It's your shirt."

Constance sat down, smiling again.

"Thanks, daddy."

On Monday Gregory did his work and went to the small park to eat his lunch. Fred and Gene were running as usual. Gregory had not spoken to them since asking about his charley horse, but now Fred nodded occasionally.

Gregory was not going to run that day, but when he got home he found himself changing into his running clothes. Might as well.

As he ran around the lake, Gregory thought about his running. He had been running for more than two years now, and he was running no faster than he had been a month or so after he had begun. He ran a lot more easily now, and as he started his third circuit of the lake he realized that where once he had thought four miles was a lot, he was now accepting six miles as standard, and could run eight, or surely ten, easily.

He thought about Fred and Gene. Had they been in the Memorial Day run? He did not know their last names so could not check. Maybe they were Track Club members. They did run fast.

They were thin. How tall? Gregory guessed that they were near five-eleven. Weight? One-forty, maybe. The more Gregory examined Fred and Gene with his mind's eye, the thinner they seemed. Skin and bones. With muscles. They were running-machines.

After Gregory took his shower, he pulled the bathroom scales out from behind the toilet bowl. They were seldom used. Elizabeth said she did not want to know how much she weighed. Gregory had weighed himself a few months after he started running, out of curiosity, but his weight had not changed. It had been perhaps a year and half since then.

Gregory stepped up on the scales. The dial bounced to a stop at 179. How was that possible? Gregory was as shocked as he had been when he found that he had run the race at more than nine minutes a mile. Now he was nine, no eight, it had really been 171, he was eight pounds heavier than when he started running. You would have thought he would have lost some weight with all that running.

Gregory examined the scales at rest. If anything, they were off on the light side. Gregory turned the adjustment until the line exactly bisected the zero. Then he stepped up again. This time the dial read 180. He stepped off and then on again: 180.

Gregory toweled the steam off the full-length mirror and looked at himself. His legs were large, but nicely muscled. They always had been, and with running, they were hard as rock. His stomach was full in front, but still you could not exactly say he had a pot. It was more like a rubber tire, extending around the back. He did not look, he thought, much different from when he was 170. Or 160, for that matter.

But it was a lot of weight to carry around. When he played ball in high school, he weighed 140. He had his full growth then, too. He was carrying forty pounds more now.

It stood to reason, Gregory thought, both that he did not need to carry that extra forty pounds, and that carrying it surely slowed his running.

"I don't want any dessert," he said at the end of dinner.

"Why not?" Elizabeth said, alert.

Gregory hesitated. "Well, I don't want any ice cream tonight."

"We've got doughnuts," Elizabeth said, going to the cupboard for the package.

"I thought I'd lose some weight," Gregory blurted out.

Elizabeth sat back down. "But you're not too heavy," she protested. She took a doughnut for herself and pushed the package toward Gregory.

Gregory ignored the doughnuts.

"You're not fat at all," Elizabeth said. She lit a cigarette, forgetting to blow the smoke away from Gregory. "Most men your age are a lot heavier than you are. And you do all that running."

"Yes, you see . . ." Gregory began. He started again. "The

running does help, that is, my weight is distributed better, and I'm fit, but . . ."

"But what?" Elizabeth asked, her lips and eyes scornful.

"Well, most runners are not this heavy," Gregory said dully.

"But you're not a runner!" Elizabeth burst out laughing. She started coughing and choked out, "I mean you're not *really* a runner. Why should you lose weight?"

Gregory slumped and shrugged his shoulders. He wished that Elizabeth had quit smoking when he did. She recovered, shook her head at him in amusement. She took another doughnut, offered it to him, and laughed again when he refused.

Elizabeth was amused all evening. Around ten she popped corn, and grinned when Gregory automatically accepted his bowl, then put it aside after eating a handful.

In bed she snuggled and said, "My old runner."

Gregory had been prepared for that, and tried not to go rigid when she repeated it.

While waiting to check out at the supermarket, Gregory had often idly read over the titles of little thirty-five cent booklets on a rack there. One of them was titled *31 Diets*. The next evening on the way home from work, Gregory detoured by the supermarket. He bought a case of diet Pepsi, and the booklet, *31 Diets*.

He sat in the car skimming through the booklet. He was hungry, having skipped lunch, and none of the diets were going to solve that problem. He did not like most of the diets. What looked best was the cottage cheese and grapefruit diet. He liked cottage cheese and grapefruit. He went back into the supermarket to buy two cartons of cottage cheese and a bag of grapefruit. There was a bottle of multi-vitamin capsules in the medicine cabinet at home that Elizabeth had once bought, but no one used. He would take one of those a day for supplement.

Gregory was pleased to find that the twins approved of his diet. They discussed it with him, and suggested that he could eat lots of lettuce, celery, and carrots, which were good for him but did not have many calories.

Elizabeth ostentatiously put the food that she had prepared for Gregory's dinner down the garbage disposal. Gregory hated that noise even more than the vacuum cleaner, and usually Elizabeth waited until he was out of the kitchen to use the disposal.

She collected his grapefruit rinds, looking down at him derisively, and put them down the garbage disposal, too.

Nevertheless, Gregory stuck to it. He was elated to see that he lost three pounds the first day. Then he lost a pound a day for two more days, but then the scales stuck at 175 for the next four days. After that his weight went down about half a pound a day, although not day by day.

After two weeks, Gregory was down to 170. He was getting very sick of cottage cheese, grapefruit, and what Elizabeth called rabbit food. He had lost ten pounds. But he was starving.

"Let's go to Shakey's Pizza for dinner tonight."

It was Gregory's suggestion, at the breakfast table. Ever since the Memorial Day Run he had been getting up in time to eat with Elizabeth and the twins.

"Well, I say," Elizabeth said sarcastically.

"Sure," Constance put in, "you need a break from your diet."

If how he felt after his evening run was any sign, Gregory's diet was indeed working. He felt weak while showering that evening, but was buoyed up by the thought of pizza.

At Shakey's they ordered two giant specials. Gregory got a pitcher of beer—his first in two weeks—and root beer for the twins.

Nothing had ever tasted so good. Gregory gorged.

Later that evening, Gregory decided he might as well live it up, so he ate buttered popcorn and drank more beer with Elizabeth. Just before going to bed, they finished half a Sara Lee strawberry cheesecake. They then made love for the first time in two weeks, the first time since Gregory had started his diet.

The next morning Gregory could not believe his eyes. He weighed 176. In one evening of eating he had put on six pounds.

He stepped up and down on the scales several times. Six pounds.

Gregory dressed grimly. It was probably mostly water, he thought. He had had a lot of beer, and they say that you can hold a lot of water in your cells. He would not drink any more beer. He had never liked it that much, anyway. He had got into the habit of drinking it in the army, and Elizabeth liked it. Ok, no more beer. He would cut down on the diet Pepsi, also. That would be harder. He did not much like the cloying taste of the saccharin or whatever sweetener they used, but Pepsi remained his all-time favorite drink. He could still remember how big the bottle had seemed to him when he was quite small.

He would quit inflating his weight with water. He would cut down on the liquids.

He was pleased to see that his weight was down to 173 the next day. But it took ten days to get back down to 170 again. Gregory hung on.

The third week A.P. (after pizza) Gregory began to have another problem. It was almost unnoticeable at first, yet he knew it was there, a faint tickle in his groin. Then it became a definite itch. Three days later it was undeniable, and he noticed spots on the front of his shorts. The next day there was a slow, but steady yellow discharge, and at the office he had to go to the Men's Room to stuff some Kleenex into his shorts to keep from spotting his trousers.

Gonorrhea? These were certainly the symptoms. But Gregory had slept with no woman but Elizabeth since they were married. Toilet seat? He knew that was nonsense. Elizabeth? That seemed absurd.

Gregory looked in the phone book. He could not go to their regular doctor. He dialed the first urologist on the list.

"Could I possibly get an appointment soon?"

"What specifically is your problem?" It was the voice of a very young woman.

"Uh, well," Gregory said, dropping his voice, "I have this

discharge, and I was wondering if I could stop by later this afternoon?" He ended in a rush.

"No, but we could fit you in first thing in the morning, say nine-thirty."

"All right," Gregory agreed. He told his work staff he would be late the next day.

All evening Gregory worried about concealing his condition from Elizabeth. However, they had not made love since the pizza night—that was another puzzle, maybe it was related to abstinence, they had been so heavy there for the last two years—and she did not notice that he was wearing his jockey shorts stuffed with Kleenex under his pajamas.

The urologist was a cynical looking old man. He listened to Gregory's description without comment. He was rough.

"This won't be comfortable," he said, pulling on a rubber glove. "Bend over."

Gregory tensed.

"Your prostate is in good shape, anyway," the urologist said. "Now I'll do it again to get a good discharge." The doctor caught a smear on a microscope slide. Gregory left a urine sample, and the young nurse smilingly took a blood sample.

"Stop by tomorrow and we'll see," the doctor said.

Gregory did not run that evening.

Next morning the doctor said, "You've got a bad urinary infection, but no VD. We'll give you a penicillin shot and a prescription for antibiotics. Now these will clear it up in a day or two, but you take all these pills, the full ten days. And drink about a gallon of water a day. If it comes back, you come back."

Gregory was dismissed. The nurse gave him the penicillin shot in his hip, and handed him the prescription and the bill. Gregory wrote out a check, started to go out the door, then turned back.

"How did I get this?" he asked the nurse.

"Well, I don't know," she giggled. "Sit down, I'll ask the doctor."

After a few minutes the nurse ushered Gregory into the urologist's office. He looked up, bored.

"You said drink a lot of water," Gregory said. "I've been on a diet and haven't been drinking much."

"How much?"

"Well, really very little. A cup of coffee in the morning. Nothing at noon. A diet Pepsi at dinner."

"And you wonder why you got a urinary infection, do you?" the doctor said dryly.

Gregory had already figured it out, but had to listen as the doctor explained sarcastically about the function of the kidneys in filtering out poisons. "If there isn't enough water flow, then you get infected. It's as simple as that. Your body has to have water. You drink at least eight big glasses a day. More. Keep it running through. You did a foolish thing." The doctor turned back to his desk.

Gregory remained seated. "But I do want to lose weight."

"What for?" the doctor asked. "You look healthy enough."

"I've been eating mostly cottage cheese and grapefruit," Gregory went on stubbornly. He had felt stupid up to now, but he was not going to be intimidated by someone with as big a pot belly as this doctor.

"Foolish again," the doctor said. "Those crank diets make a lot of money for me. You've got to have a balanced diet. Ask the nurse to give you the 1200 calorie diet plan when you go out."

Gregory got up to go.

"Most people gain back more than they lose, anyway," was the doctor's parting shot.

The diet plan was printed on a folded sheet of paper. Unlike the doctor, its author was full of encouragement and hope. Everything was eminently reasonable. You ate a varied and balanced diet of all the regular foods. You took a multi-vitamin capsule every day (Gregory congratulated himself on this score at least), you drank a lot of water, and once you get underway with the prepared diet, you began counting calories and designing your own meals. When you reached your desired weight (the chart said that a man Gregory's age and height should weigh 154, which was a pleasant surprise), you slowly increase your caloric intake until you figure out what your maintenance diet is. Then you continue counting calories and eat only enough to maintain your weight.

Eminently reasonable. Fad diets were bad both nutritionally and because they do not prepare you to cut down on regular food after the diet is over. So you go back to the old routine and balloon again.

Gregory drank in this information. How could he have been so stupid?

Well, he had it right now. On the way home that evening he stopped at the supermarket to pick up a few items for the planned diet, and this time he bought the little booklet titled *Calorie Counter*. This really appealed to him. He liked the notion of counting calories. On impulse he tossed in a small notebook, for keeping records.

7

The twins' graduation from high school had more impact on Gregory and Elizabeth than anything previously in their married lives. Not the twins' birth, nor any illnesses. There had been no financial difficulties, no serious emotional upsets, and although the twins had smoked marijuana, Donald had come home drunk, Constance had been discovered taking birth control pills—all of this had been taken in stride. At the graduation ceremony, Gregory and Elizabeth sat holding hands. Tears slid openly down Gregory's cheeks, and before the parents kissed the twins, they kissed each other.

The twins had said for years that they wanted to go to the University of Minnesota, but in their last year of high school they changed their minds. On a vacation in the west, Donald had decided he liked the mountains, and that he wanted to be an engineer. He had been accepted at the Colorado School of Mines. But he was not waiting until fall to go. With a friend, he was leaving the following week to hike—he said climb, which made Elizabeth shudder—in the mountains all summer. Constance had fallen in love with the St. Olaf campus in Northfield, not far from where Gregory had grown up in Northwood. Gregory's parents were pleased that Constance was going to a Lutheran college and would be close to them. It pleased Gregory, also, strangely he thought, for he had—since the army—felt indifferent to his home town, to his religion, and even to his parents. Constance was leaving within the week also, to be a counselor at Camp White Cloud on Happy Jack Lake in northern Minnesota.

Gregory and Elizabeth would be alone and the house would be quiet for the first time in eighteen years.

On Monday, Gregory took the afternoon off and arrived home early. The twins were packing, and Elizabeth was exasperated by the disruption. Gregory got a diet Pepsi from the refrigerator and went up to sit at the top of the stairs. Both Donald and Constance were stacking in the hall what they intended to take. Donald was making two piles, one for sending to school, the other for summer. Constance, despite Elizabeth's protests that she would be back a week before classes started at St. Olaf, was doing the same. Gregory watched in amusement.

"Hey, take a break," Gregory said. Elizabeth sat down beside him on the stairs at once, but the twins slowed only when Gregory added, "I've got something to tell you."

Gregory waited and then went on. "Well, you know for years we've been talking about taking a Windjammer Cruise ..."

"Oh, daddy," Constance wailed, "that's not fair. You know we can't go ..." She stopped when she saw Donald looking at her sternly. He was taking on college-man airs already.

"What, what?" Gregory said with mock surprise. "You mean you have other plans?"

Elizabeth giggled.

"Yeah," Constance said. "Other plans. But, oh daddy, it's a great idea. Are you really going?"

"Yep," Gregory said, reaching for some folders in his hip pocket. I just arranged it all today. Three weeks in the Caribbean. Johanson said it would be fine," he said, in reply to Elizabeth's unspoken question. "We haven't taken a long vacation in years, and he said to go ahead. What do you think, Elizabeth?" He had not thought before to ask her if she really wanted to go.

"Of course," she said, kissing him.

"Well," Gregory said, standing up, "at least we don't have to pack in this uproar. We don't leave until June twentieth. I almost didn't get us on at all, but a couple canceled yesterday and we just got in." He looked down at Elizabeth, pleased—and something he had not expected, also relieved—that she was pleased.

"Well," he said, "I'm going to take a long run now. There won't be much of that on the water."

During the next few days Gregory and Elizabeth busied themselves with their own plans and packing, and thus survived the twins' leavetaking.

"They'll be here only on visits from now on," Elizabeth said once.

Another time Gregory said, "And later on they may think about us and about coming to see us as little as I do about my own parents."

June twentieth came quickly enough. Gregory and Elizabeth took a regular airline flight to Miami, and transferred there to a charter flight in a small plane that held the fourteen Windjammer passengers for Bermuda. Gregory noticed that only one other couple was nearly as old as he and Elizabeth, the rest apparently being in their twenties. But everyone was friendly, and Gregory soon forgot his age.

Everything sparkled in the Caribbean sun, the air, the water over many shades of deep blue, the sand, and even the brass on the schooner. Compared to the little skiffs back home on the lake, this was a real ship, three masts, little colored flags snapping in the breeze.

Elizabeth caught her breath and squeezed Gregory's hand. "Oh," she said, "it will be fun."

Gregory grinned broadly, unsteady in his new sneakers as he went up the flimsy ramp onto the deck. Although they had talked about taking a Windjammer Cruise for years, he doubted that they had been quite serious. He had signed up on an impulse. It had been a good one.

The first days were like dreams. Some of the work of sailing was hard, and Gregory felt awkward, although he knew more than many of the others. His back burned, he got rope burns on his hands, and he forgot the world of accounting completely. Elizabeth, too, pitched in with the sailing, more than any of the other women. She was the captain's favorite, and he often called on her to do heavy work that someone else might have thought to ask of a man.

The food was exotic, everyone drank too much, and Gregory went off his maintenance diet. He had not maintained it very well, anyway. It had been easy enough—he discovered—to stay on the diet once he got started. The chart said he should be 154, but since he had started at 180, he really could not stop there. He lost thirty pounds for round measure, and because he liked the thought of being able to gain four pounds and still not be overweight. He had not watched very carefully after that, and just before the cruise he had weighed himself. It was three months since the end of his diet and he had gained seven pounds. Well, three pounds overweight. He could lose that. But not on the Windjammer Cruise, not while having the time of his life.

Gregory's sexual appetite revived, and although Elizabeth chided him that it was because of all the nearly naked female flesh around, she responded eagerly. The tiny cabins were private in intent, but the partitions were very thin. No one could be in doubt about the aphrodisiac effect of ship and sun and sea.

One evening they were anchored in a beautiful isolated bay. The water was as clear as air to sand below. Their schooner was the only sign of human beings. They ate lobster for dinner and sat talking and drinking until late. Gregory hated to go to bed, but supposed he should, so finally he and Elizabeth went to their cabin. It was such a quiet, subdued night that they did not make love.

There was a scratching at the door. Gregory could not figure out how long he had been asleep, it seemed that he had just dozed off.

"It is zee night," someone said in a loud stage whisper through the slats in the door, "zee night of zee traditional nude swim. Come!" There was a pause. "You hear me?"

"Yes," Gregory replied automatically. He could feel that Elizabeth was wide awake beside him. Gregory sighed. It was for the younger ones. He lay back.

"Well?" Elizabeth said, poking him.

"Well, what?"

"Aren't we going?"

"I'd be embarrassed," Gregory said.

Elizabeth giggled. "So would I." Then she said, "But if that's what they do, shouldn't we do it? I mean, isn't it part of it?"

Elizabeth had not asked how much the cruise was costing. She seldom bothered about prices. Knowing the cost, Gregory was inclined to think that they ought to get their money's worth. It would be exciting. He would not mind. Elizabeth had drunk quite a lot and was still tipsy. She would probably be embarrassed in the morning. So what?

"All right," Gregory said, and swung out of the bunk. He was already nude, which seemed the proper way to sleep in the romantic Caribbean. Elizabeth stood beside him in a thin negligee.

"What do we do?" she asked.

"Take that off," Gregory said.

Elizabeth giggled and slid the negligee over her head.

"Now what?"

Gregory did not know. They had terry cloth robes for after swimming, so he handed one to Elizabeth and put one on himself. They peeked out the door, and then went hesitantly up on deck.

Nothing was happening. Only a few people were there, also in robes. They seemed to be as timid as Gregory was. After twenty minutes, however, most of the couples had arrived. They talked quietly. The captain and the young crew members were there, too.

It was late. A slab of moon had lifted over the water, giving enough light to see by, but nothing like the brilliance of the full moon seven nights ago.

Then a girl standing near the bow of the schooner said loudly, "So who's chicken?" She dropped her robe, posed for a moment, her white flesh glowing against the blue-black sky, then dived into the sea.

Suddenly everyone was laughing and talking loudly. The captain came up and gave Gregory a shove. "Into the water, old man!"

Gregory awkwardly took off his robe, stepped quickly to the rail, and dived overboard. It was not as though he had not spent his youth swimming nude in the river near Northwood. Just before he hit the water he remembered to cup one hand between his legs for protection. The water was warm and caressed his entire body. One ought always to swim nude.

Gregory went deep. He swam as far as he could underwater before he had to surface. He was more than fifty yards from the schooner. The others were staying close under the bow. Gregory heard Elizabeth's throaty laughter. One of the things that had attracted him to her when they first met was the spontaneous, uninhibited laugh. You could only call it a belly laugh, the sort that wells up from the whole being when you tickle a baby. Elizabeth had retained it at eighteen, and she had it still. It had even grown deeper over the years, as she got more belly, Gregory grinned. He never heard that laugh without smiling, no matter how annoyed he might be with Elizabeth.

Gregory rolled onto his back and lazily circled the schooner. He had seldom felt so content and whole. In the last ten days his life had been stripped to sun and sea. There was the schooner, and off over there a beach, and out there nothing. It was too simple to be real, but to Gregory now the accounting office was what seemed unreal. He had been going to that office for just over twenty years. He frowned, but then pushed aside thoughts of the office, or rather, they faded into the night.

Suddenly firm hands on his shoulders pushed him under.

"Say, Greg, you can't catch me."

Gregory started out after the girl. It was Debbie, the one who had dived in first.

It turned out that she was right. Gregory was a strong swimmer, and had swum around and across the lake at home times beyond counting. Debbie, however, had probably been a college swimmer. Gregory kept after her with his dogged crawl stroke, but he knew he would catch her only if she wanted him to. They swam steadily for what seemed a long time. Then Debbie went under in a surface dive at full speed. Gregory pulled up and treaded water. It was hard to estimate in the moonlight how far they were from the schooner. Five hundred yards? Gregory was not worried about the distance, he was sure he could swim all night. And this warm Caribbean salt water was incredibly buoyant compared to the cold sterile waters of Minnesota.

Debbie surfaced right in front of him.

"Say, you're all right, old man," she said in mock seriousness. "I thought you might catch me."

Gregory grinned at the teasing.

"It's beautiful," he said, thinking of the night, but with awareness of Debbie's slim body in the water with him.

Debbie glanced down, threw her arms above her head to plunge down deep feet first, then shot straight up out of the water almost as high as her hips before splashing down again.

"It is, it is," she cried. "Let's swim to the beach." She started off without waiting for Gregory to agree.

They appeared to be about halfway there already. Gregory hesitated and then started after Debbie. He was breathless but not tired when his hands touched the sand. There were practically no waves. Debbie stood in the knee-deep water waiting for him.

"Come on," she reached down and took him by the hand. He stood up and they ran with high steps through the water to the shore.

Debbie turned and nestled against him. He kissed her upturned face.

"Now try to catch me," she said, breaking away to run down the beach.

Gregory laughed out loud. This was his element. He ran easily up to her, kept alongside, swept in a big circle around her, sped ahead, then turned and stopped with arms outstretched to block her path. She ran right into him, pushing him over and landing on top of him.

"Amazing," she said, sitting straddled on his stomach. "You must be a jogger."

She traced her finger down his nose, then hunched down on top of him.

"Aren't you going to make love to me?" she whispered in his ear.

"It appears," Gregory said, "that we're in position the other way around."

"So it does, yes it does," Debbie said. She reached behind her back and took hold of Gregory. "And everything seems to be in order. Well, you can run and swim, let's see . . ."

Gregory lay back and hung on, but Debbie made him claw the sand.

When they caught their breath, Gregory said, "That was very nice . . . Debbie . . . that was so very nice of you."

She nestled on top of him. "You mean because you're a dirty old man and I'm a sweet young thing? Well, I'm beginning to think maybe you're not so old." Then she pushed her palms down on his chest and rocked over to crouch beside him, looking at him carefully. "But you certainly are dirty," she said, deliberately dribbling sand across his belly and down between his legs.

Gregory reared up. Debbie ran toward the water, shrieking with laughter. Gregory started after her, then stopped. He looked around. A sandy beach, some dry grasses rustling in a barely perceptible breeze, sparse trees farther back. Half a moon.

Debbie was treading water, waiting for him. Gregory swam out to her. She threw her arms around him and they sank under. Then they swam together back to the schooner, talking about whatever crossed Debbie's mind.

Later all that Gregory could remember of the conversation was that Debbie had exclaimed, "Isn't it a marvelous cruise?" and had gone on to say something else by the time Gregory could say that yes, it was.

They were hooted when they got back to the schooner. Debbie climbed up the ladder with total aplomb, donning without haste the robe that was handed to her. Gregory tried to be as blasé, and seemed so to the others.

"You swam all the way to shore and back?" someone said with amazement.

"That's nothing," Elizabeth's strong voice put it. Gregory had refrained from looking around for her, but now saw her sitting in a lounge chair beside the captain, a tall drink in her hand. "Greggie-boy's a runner," Elizabeth went on, with some pride in her voice. She never actually drank too much, that is, she could hold a great deal without showing it much. Now she went on to exaggerate Gregory's running abilities in a way that she would not do if she were cold sober.

They watched the sun rise, and then went to bed to sleep off the night. The room was stuffy when Gregory woke sometime after noon. He had a hangover. The day was still and hot.

In mid-afternoon the captain used the engine to see if they could get out where there might be some wind. The day passed and then there were only five more left. The cruise was effectively over and Gregory started thinking about the office.

One relief was that Debbie made nothing special of their long swim, neither avoiding Gregory nor seeking him out. She had been friendly before. Now she was even nicer, both to him and to Elizabeth, who liked her. Sometimes when talking to him, Debbie put her hand on Gregory's arm or chest. This thrilled him, but seemed unpremeditated, and led to nothing further. Gregory had disapproved greatly when he found out that Constance was taking birth control pills, but Elizabeth had talked him out of showing it. Now he thought that if Constance had a healthy a view of sex as Debbie, then surely it was all right. Whether or not Constance was like Debbie, Gregory would never know.

When they returned to Minneapolis, Elizabeth was quite content to settle into life together without the twins. Gregory was restless. He started to diet again, but without cutting down much, because Elizabeth had become very sensitive about it.

What troubled Gregory was the situation at the office. Three years ago it had been assumed that he would soon be promoted to a vice-presidency. It had not happened yet. Again, it was not the money, for he needed no increase. But it was a matter of progress, of advancement appropriate to his contribution, his ability, his years concerned with central company matters. It was a small firm, and Johanson called most of the shots. So when Gregory had gone in to ask about taking off for nearly four weeks on such short notice, he thought to ask about the promotion.

Johanson, who had been magnanimous about Gregory's taking time off on such short notice, turned his pale Scandinavian profile to the side at the question.

"You didn't ask," Johanson said.

"What?" Gregory was puzzled.

"When the time came, you didn't ask to be promoted," Johanson said.

"But I thought you understood . . ."

"Yes," Johanson went slowly, "I know we had discussed it, and I knew you wanted it. But it wasn't quite time." Johanson locked his big hands together and twisted them. He looked directly at Gregory. "But when the time came, you seemed to have forgotten it. Your mind seemed to be on something else." Johanson looked away again. "You didn't ask."

Johanson was right, of course. Gregory had not forgotten about the vice-presidency, but he just had not thought to bring it up for a long time, not until now. It was very awkward.

"Joe, my work . . ."

"Oh, your work is fine," Johanson said vehemently. He turned back to face Gregory again, a broad smile on his face. "Your work has always been first-rate, we all know that. Look," he went on, radiating joviality, "go take your cruise. You can use it. I wish I could go along." (Gregory knew the last was false, Johanson hated water.) "We can talk about this again when you get back."

When Gregory got back he found that Brown, the young man who had taken over his work when he was away, now retained some of the more crucial parts of it. Johanson said something meaningless about the shift, and Gregory did not pursue it. Nothing further was said about the vice-presidency.

There had also been the unpleasantness with Elizabeth. She had not said anything about Gregory's nude swim with Debbie until they got back to Miami. They had to stay overnight to catch a morning flight back to Minneapolis, and they felt so deflated that they simply stayed at the airport Holiday Inn without even going to town for dinner. Then even Elizabeth almost could not finish the plastic motel food. She called her parents and argued about not being able to stop for a few days. The television set in their room did not work well. They went to bed early.

Gregory lay on his back with his hands behind his head, thinking vague thoughts. He wondered why he did not really care about the vice-presidency. Not very long ago he would have been quite disturbed at not getting what he knew was his due. Now his speculation about what was on Johanson's mind bored him. Johanson had nothing but accounting on his mind, probably.

It would be good to get back to running. Gregory's legs felt still and unused to solid ground.

"Did you and Debbie . . .?" Elizabeth asked.

Gregory turned to her in the darkness, put his hand on her hip. "Yes, but . . ."

"Well, good," Elizabeth said loudly. "Don't apologize. "I'm glad. I thought maybe you wouldn't for some stupid reason." She struggled to a sitting position and lit a cigarette.

"And the captain . . .?" Gregory asked.

Elizabeth laughed and coughed.

"The captain!? You ninny. The *captain*. How could you miss that? Didn't you know that he was just one of us girls?" Her deep laughter filled the room. She had controlled her cough.

"No." Gregory had not noticed. But now that he thought about it, it seemed right. Some of the boys in the crew had been somewhat fey.

"How was it?" Elizabeth asked.

"What?" Gregory said, still bemused with the thought of the captain.

"Debbie."

"Oh." Gregory had not wanted to analyze it. What he remembered was how slight her body had been. She had bent like a willow and his arms had overlapped around her. Her small breasts had been pointed and firm, her arms and legs compact, tight.

"Well . . . how was it?

"Fine," Gregory said. But Elizabeth wanted more. "It was very nice." Gregory paused. Elizabeth would not let him off. Gregory told her briefly, how they had swum to the beach, how Debbie had run him down, that she had been on top of him.

"And you liked it, eh?" Elizabeth said, stubbing out her cigarette.

Some of it had come back to Gregory. "Yes," he said distractedly, "Yes, I liked it."

The talk had aroused Gregory. He leaned over to caress Elizabeth.

Elizabeth slapped him full in the face. She had a heavy arm. Gregory's ear rang, his cheek burned, and tears came to his eyes.

"Oh, Greggie!" Elizabeth cried, engulfing him in her arms and pulling him down on top on her. I'm sorry, I didn't mean to do that. I don't care. It was such a wonderful cruise. I'm so miserable." Elizabeth sobbed.

Gregory ministered to her urgent need. He was always capable of that, even now, his face smarting from the only time she ever hit him, his mind a blank about the true cause of her anger and misery.

Elizabeth tensed, her sobs now a whimper.

"Ahhh," she arched, shuddered, relaxed.

"Now you, Greggie," she said in a small voice. Gregory went on to his release with Elizabeth whispering that she loved him.

"Me, too," he said in a strangulated voice. "I love you, too."

Elizabeth sighed and Gregory rolled over so she could get a cigarette.

"How was it?" Elizabeth asked.

"Fine," Gregory said instantly. "It was very good."

Elizabeth smoked quietly while Gregory pretended to drift off to sleep.

Later he heard Elizabeth crying softly beside him. He turned and nestled against her, throwing an arm over her hip as he always did.

She gripped his arm, pressing him to her.

"Oh, Greggie," she said. "I'm so . . ., I'm so . . ., oh, I'm so fat and ugly and old."

"I love you," Gregory said.

Elizabeth finally went to sleep.

Gregory drifted in and out of consciousness the rest of the night. She was fat. She drank a lot. He had not noticed before he quit drinking beer, but then he figured out that she drank at least a six-pack or more a day. He said nothing to her about it. She was not ugly. She had never been pretty, but her face was handsome. She laughed a lot. And they were both getting old, he supposed, although forty-five (no, was he not forty-six?) was not considered old these days. He did not feel old. He felt fine.

As for being miserable, he supposed he could see why she might be. It was probably a delayed reaction to the twins leaving. They had been her life. Now what did she have to do? Play bridge once a week. Drink beer, eat popcorn, watch television every night. Putter in the garden a bit. Clean the house.

Gregory knew he could not just let it go at the office. However, there was no easy way to bring it up. Johanson was always jolly with Gregory now. He seemed both more friendly and more distant than before. In the past, Johanson had confided in Gregory. He now no longer showed Gregory when he was down, and Gregory had more of a feeling that things were right when Johanson showed when he was down.

A month went by. Then, after sporadic postcards, there was a long letter from Donald. He and his friend had joined two other climbers to set up camp outside Aspen, Colorado. Lots of girls in Aspen, he had put in parenthetically. They had climbed the Maroon Bells once, and were preparing to do it by a more difficult route.

Toward the end of the letter, Donald wrote:

> Look, I know you've had one vacation, but why not have another? Come to Aspen. It's a very pretty place. Expensive, but you could bring the big tent and set up at our base camp and save money that way. You could blow it on the fancy restaurants in Aspen. Why don't you? You liked the mountains when we were out here three years ago. Live it up. Mom, there are lots of wild flowers, you could hike. Dad, you could see if you could run up these old mountain roads. You could even do some climbing, yes, how about that? Dad, come on and we'll teach you how to climb.

There were detailed instructions on how to reach the base camp.

Elizabeth was smiling when she handed the letter to Gregory. He read it, and then read the last part again. He had liked the mountains, and the idea of camping out awhile gripped him. He would like to run in the mountains. Who knows, maybe he would even like to learn to climb?

He turned eagerly to Elizabeth, "Well?"

Elizabeth looked at him in amazement. "But we've already had our vacation."

"It doesn't matter. Johanson won't care. I'd really like to go."

Elizabeth sat at the kitchen table, studying Gregory.

"Hunh-unh," she shook her head, her expression neutral. "I've had my fling. You go right ahead if you want to. I'm sitting right here. And get me a beer, since you're up."

Gregory got the beer out of the refrigerator and unfastened his tie as he walked upstairs to get into his running clothes. Should he go? Why not? Well, what would old Johanson think? Old Johanson. Johanson was five years older than Gregory. Fifty, or so. He had always seemed fifty. Gregory wondered how old Johanson felt now that he really was fifty.

Gregory had been running eight miles since he got back. Tonight without noticing, he circled the lake five times, ten miles.

The next morning Gregory went first thing into Johanson's office.

"I'd like to take another week or ten days leave to go out to Colorado to see my boy," he said without preliminaries.

Johanson was startled. At least he was not jovial.

"But you've just . . ." he began. "I mean . . ." He looked at Gregory's grim face. "Well, look," Johanson went on, "I suppose it will be all right. It will put a little strain on us. Other people are taking vacations, too," he said sternly. "But I suppose Brown could take over again."

Gregory nodded firmly. Brown was very deferential to Gregory, as he should be, taking over his work. Brown had also made a point of letting everyone in the office know that he did not plan to take a vacation this summer.

"Yes," Johanson said, making up his mind. "It'll be all right. Take two weeks if need be," he added solicitously.

Gregory realized that Johanson thought that he was going to Colorado to straighten out some trouble Donald had gotten into. Good, let him think that. It saved them all the difficulty of trying to figure out just why Gregory was going.

Elizabeth did not question it. She helped Gregory pack, and made only a few obligatory sarcastic remarks. She drove him to the airport, pecked him on the cheek, and told him to be careful.

He flew to Denver, took a bus to Aspen, and was glad after a quarter of a mile of hiking up the mountain road that some kids in an old pickup truck offered him a ride. They dropped him at the landmark—a large boulder with JESUS SAVES spray-painted on it.

Gregory hoisted his pack onto his back. He had tried to cut it down, but it still weighed sixty-five pounds. There was a trail. Donald had said that it was only about a mile. He had not mentioned that it was up.

Gregory took it easy. He was a little short of breath, so rested often. He had not been bothered by the altitude when they visited the mountains before, and he did not think it was bothering him now.

Gregory reached the camp with no trouble by mid-afternoon. There was no one there, but he recognized some of Donald's gear, so he set up his tent at a slight distance from the other two tents. He had purchased a new lightweight tent just for this trip. He had some difficulty adjusting the rain fly, but was happy to be doing it. He took a long time unpacking, arranging. He read a chapter of a mystery novel, and then decided to take a hike.

It was a different sun from that of the Caribbean, not so hot, but it had burned him on the hike up the trail, despite his tan. He should have brought a hat. He went to the tent to get the visor he wore when running on sunny days. As an afterthought, he arranged a bandanna over his head under the visor.

When he got back there was still no one in camp. At dusk he prepared a meal for himself. There was a gasoline lantern by the tents, so he lit it and settled down to read. He had just finished the book when he heard the boys returning.

They were prepared to be angry, but before the others could say anything, Donald shouted, "Dad, what are you doing here?"

Gregory's heart sank, but as he mumbled an excuse, Donald went on.

"Hey, that's just great! I never thought for a minute you'd come. But you did. That's great! Where's mom?" Donald looked over at Gregory's small tent. "Didn't come, eh? That's too bad." Without pausing Donald went on, "I'm starved, when do we eat?"

The other three had already started preparations. As soon as Donald slowed down from the surprise, he introduced the two Gregory had not met before. They were from California. Donald was formal about it, and in general was rather quiet and shy. Not having seen him for more than two months, Gregory was struck by the reflection of his own mannerisms in his son.

As they ate, they told Gregory of the day's climb. It had been more than they had anticipated, which is why they had returned so late. Gregory had already surmised from their well-used ropes and gear that they were not just walking up the slopes. But despite having read a number of mountain climbing books, he did not entirely follow their happy telling of the story of the climb. It was to each other, and for themselves, as much as to inform Gregory.

After they had eaten, they went to bed. Gregory had some trouble getting to sleep. That was probably the altitude. He was relieved that Donald was pleased to see him.

The next morning Gregory awoke early. There was no sound from the boys, so he put on his running gear. There was a chill in the air, but it was against the sun that he put on a turtle-necked jersey. He decided he could wear shorts if he also wore new knee socks that would stay up.

He jogged slowly down the trail to the road, going carefully to cut down on the shock to his knees. Donald had said that it was five miles to the edge of town. Thinking of the altitude, Gregory ran slowly. It was generally downhill. When he reached Aspen, he turned and started back up. This was more strenuous and he slowed down more, but he felt fine. When he reached the turnoff, he continued up the trail. Here, finally, he was forced to a walk and his breath came heavily, but he kept on.

The boys were cooking breakfast. Gregory was distressed to see that the look on Donald's face was naked pride in his father, the runner. Gregory got a towel and some clothes from his tent and went over to the shallow stream that was tumbling down beside their camp. He splashed himself with the icy water, toweled off and dressed, and then joined the boys for pancakes. He was famished. There goes the diet again.

"We're just going over to that face," Donald indicated after breakfast, "to work on technique. No real climbing today. You want to come along?"

Gregory nodded.

When they reached the base of the cliff, a broken wall of rock a few hundred feet high, with many vertical cracks lining it, Gregory asked, "Don't you have any hammers and pitons?"

"Sure," Donald said, "we have some back at the tent. But pitons hurt the rock. We use these." He held up a handful of metal wedges, strung with different colored bands of webbing. "Chocks," Donald said. "Here, I'll show you."

And so without ever discussing it, Gregory began to learn the rudiments of modern rock climbing. Before the end of the day he had learned to rappel, and he had climbed stretches of more than a hundred feet up several different portions of the wall. His teachers were competent and confident. Gregory was worried about the exposure at first, but he could see that they were careful always to protect him, tied into a safety rope on belay. It was a thoroughly enjoyable day. He remembered the pleasure of teaching Donald to sail.

That evening the boys discussed a long hike and difficult climb they had planned for some time. It would take three or four days. They were considering whether or not to go the next day.

"I'll stay here," Gregory said, dispelling the uncertainty he felt they had about him. "I'd like to do some climbing," he went on, "but I'd better have some more practice, and this sounds too hard, anyway. I'll do some running and get acclimatized."

Thereafter the discussion was more focused. When Gregory awoke the next morning, the boys were gone. He grinned thinking how difficult it had been for Elizabeth to get Donald up for school all those years.

This time he ran up the road, trying to figure the distance by time. But why bother with that? He would just run until he felt like turning back. His muscles were stiff from the climbing the day before, but they soon grew limber again. During the middle part of the day he read and puttered around camp, improving the fireplace. Sometime past mid-afternoon he felt restless, so put on his outfit to run down to Aspen and back. He ate an early dinner, and went to bed early. Next morning he was up at dawn.

There were many side roads, mining and forest roads, trails. Gregory explored. He ran slowly so that he did not wear himself out, an hour or two in the morning, a lazy mid-day meal, then an hour or two in the late afternoon. The fourth day he ran down to Aspen to buy some more paperback books and some oranges. The small pack he carried them in thumped on his back, but he was very fit now, and ran straight up the steep trail to camp. On the fifth day he wondered if he should worry about the boys. He did not worry, and toward dusk on the sixth day he saw them returning. He had been ready for this, and started cooking the big meal he had in readiness for them, steaks, bisquits, even a blackberry pie in a reflector oven. They ate and talked late into the night.

"How long can you stay, dad?" Donald asked him the next morning.

It had been a week. Another of those lost times, no time at all.

"Well, Johanson said to take a couple of weeks if I needed them, so why not?" Gregory said thoughtfully. His feelings were odd. Rationally he felt that he should be concerned about getting back to work, but he wanted to stay and knew he was going to.

What seemed somewhat strange to him was the firmness of this decision without any of the anxiety he might have felt in the past. It was not that he believed what he was doing was right. There was no rightness nor wrongness about it. Gregory had an entirely neutral feeling about the office. His work was there, he knew. But it did not matter.

"Great!" Donald said. "Well, let's do some real climbing today."

"Shouldn't I practice more?"

"Nah, you know enough. Only way to learn is to climb, anyway."

Another week went by. Gregory found the climbing exhilarating. At the end of the week they climbed the hard route up the Maroon Bells, something the boys had already done once. Then the two boys from California had to go back to school. Donald's friend from Minneapolis was going to the Colorado School of Mines with Donald, but they did not have to be there for another ten days. They were going to pull up stakes here to hitch-hike over to Rocky Mountain National Park where they hoped to climb the North Face of Long's Peak.

The next morning they closed camp. Gregory was quiet, and he finished first. He sat on his pack watching the two boys. When they were ready, he said, "Say, why don't I go with you? We can take the bus, I'll pay."

Donald looked uncertain. "Gee, dad, I don't know. Long's Peak . . ."

"Oh, I don't have to climb it with you," Gregory said quickly. "But I thought I might go along."

Donald was still thinking about the climb. "It's not that I think you couldn't do it technically," he mused. "We're going to try Stettner's Ledges, and they say that's a relatively easy route. But it's exposure like you've never seen before."

"Let's not worry about that now," Gregory said. "I just thought . . ."

"Sure," Donald agreed, smiling. "Sure, why not? Let's take the bus. We'll get there sooner that way, and have more time to think about it."

In the bus station Gregory called Elizabeth. He had managed to send her only one postcard.

"Just tell Johanson I've been unavoidably delayed another week."

"But what are you doing?"

"Climbing, hiking, you know, with Donald."

"But three weeks?"

"Well, you know, it may be the last time. He's going off to college and he'll change." Gregory knew that Elizabeth would accept that explanation.

"All right, if you say so," Elizabeth sighed.

"Don't tell Johanson anything else," Gregory said. "Just say that I've been unavoidably detained."

"Yes, I know," Elizabeth hardened. "Old skin head called last week, concerned about how Donald was getting along. What did you tell him?"

"Nothing," Gregory said. "He made it up himself."

"Yes, I suppose he would," Elizabeth said. "Well, if you must. And be careful."

They stayed in the climbers' camp at the base of Long's Peak for three days before the weather looked right. There were many campers about, and much hullabaloo. Gregory let Donald handle the problems of registering with the National Park Service. The Rangers examined them and their equipment, giving them a permit with noncommital expressions on their faces. Apparently it would cost plenty if you had to be rescued.

Gregory took long runs every day. They did not discuss whether or not he would try the climb.

On the fourth day they got up at three in the morning to hike up the scree to the face. By the time the sun rose they were high on the rock. The exposure was intense in places, but Gregory felt good. The climbing itself was technically easy. The weather was fine, and they progressed on the standard schedule. It was a long climb, but they expected to reach the top by noon. Then they could take the easy hike down the cable route to camp again.

Near the top Gregory sensed that the boys ahead were having some trouble. He heard scraps of intense conversation. After half an hour—the longest they had paused so far—he heard Donald say, "Easy does it now," and then his shout, "Great! We've got it." There was another wait, then Donald shouted down, "Ok, dad, your turn."

As Gregory climbed up, he saw the problem. It was an overhang, a bulge of rock that you had somehow to cling to, reach above, and pull yourself over. It looked hard enough, but what was worse was that it bulged right out over the sheer face of the giant mountain wall. There was an open drop of 2000 feet below.

When Gregory reached the overhang he stopped.

"You there?" Donald asked. He was out of sight above the bulge.

"Yeah."

"Ok, now," Donald said. "Technically it's tough, but nothing more than you can do. You're almost as tall as I am, and you have plenty of reach. The problem is that you have to depend a lot on your arms." Donald never mentioned the exposure. "Now I've got you in a good belay, and I'm tied in up here on a good wide ledge. I couldn't possibly drop you. But if you fall, there would be a little problem. What we'd have to do is lower you just a little. Look down there, see? About twenty feet down."

Gregory peered cautiously down. He was standing on a ledge about twenty inches wide, and felt safe enough except for the exposure. He now saw what the awesomeness of the great open expanse had concealed from him before. About twenty feet down was another slight bulge. A fall would be free, but you could be lowered to reach that bulge. And from there it would be a difficult, but still a quite feasible climb back up to the ledge he was standing on. It did not bear thinking about what would happen if you fell again while climbing back up to the ledge..

"Now if you need support, say so," Donald went on. "I can pull pretty hard here. And if you fall, give me plenty of warning. I'll keep you snugged up tight. There shouldn't be any problem. Ok?"

"Yeah," Gregory said in a cracked voice.

"Ok, ready."

"On belay," Gregory said.

"On belay," Donald repeated.

"Climbing."

"Climb."

There was nothing else to do. Gregory moved over beneath the bulging rock, standing straight as he had been taught, to get full traction on his feet, not leaning into the rock at an angle which might make him slide off.

He reached up, found a hold, found a second hold for his other hand, and then put out a foot. He tested all three holds as best he could, then cautiously lifted his other foot off the ledge and scratched around the base of the bulge for a place to lodge it.

There. He was momentarily secure. Three points solid, Gregory reached up over the bulge with his right hand.

"That's it," Donald said quietly. A little to your right and farther in. Feel it. That's the hold."

It didn't feel like much to Gregory. He had been expecting a crack, but this was just a low round projection. You did not so much grip it as press down on it, hoping that the friction of your hand against the rock would hold you.

"Don't pause now," Donald went on in the same quiet voice, "it's too hard on your arms. I've got you tight. Come on."

Gregory pressed down and pulled up on his right arm. He lunged up with his left arm and found nothing. He had let go with his left hand too soon, and had moved too fast. He could not believe it, but he was going to fall.

"Falling!" he croaked.

"Gotcha!" Donald's strained voice came down.

Donald had been holding so close that Gregory had not fallen far. He had merely slid down about ten feet. However, he was swinging almost free, his toes grazing the rock face, and the ledge he had been standing on was well out of reach.

"Ok, dad?"

"Yes," Gregory said. He had felt a great fright, but now he was as calm as he had ever been.

"Ok, now we've got to do this quickly and you've got to guide me, because I can't see. Ok?" Donald said.

"Ok."

"All right, I'm going to let you down slowly. You've got to tell me when to stop. And watch, don't go too far, there's too much friction on the rope, I don't think we could pull you up very far."

Gregory dropped another foot, then moved down smoothly.

"Slow," he shouted, "Slower, slower. Stop!"

Gregory's feet seemed placed fairly well on the rock now, but the rope held him too tightly for him to move freely.

"A little more."

"What?"

"More rope. Slack!"

Suddenly, Gregory was standing free. He had about three feet of slack rope. He teetered a moment, then leaned forward into the rock. There were two good holds under his hands.

"On belay!" he screamed.

"On belay," Donald yelled back. The rope pulled up snug again.

"Climbing!"

"Climb."

Gregory moved rapidly but carefully the twenty feet back up to the ledge. He was breathing heavily when he got there.

"You all right?" Donald asked.

Gregory nodded, then said, "All right."

"All right, then," Donald said, "the minute you get your wind, try again. There's no other way. And it does you no good to think about it."

"Ok," Gregory said. He took a deep breath. He was calm again.
"On belay."
"On belay."
"Climbing."
"Climb."

Gregory moved smoothly up onto the bulge. This time he spidered his body a foot higher on the bulge itself, moving one hand and then one foot at a time. Then he reached his right arm up over the bulge. Now he could raise his elbow and the hold felt a lot firmer. Donald said nothing. Gregory reached up with his left arm, his body securely held by his other three points of contact. He felt around carefully and found a projection for his left hand. He could raise his left elbow, too. Now he moved his right foot up and found a toe hold. Without pausing, he pressed up, his left leg swinging free, and he bellied over the top of the bulge.

A piece of cake.

Now he felt for the first time how tightly Donald was holding his safety rope. Gregory slid forward onto the ledge and said, "A little slack."

The look of relief that came over Donald's white face almost frightened Gregory again, but he was too elated at having made it.

"Off belay," he said, his voice cracking again.

"Off belay," Donald replied, tears in his eyes. Or perhaps it was sweat, Donald's shirt was soaked. "Beautiful, dad," he said. "Beautiful."

Gregory stood up. "Aren't we almost there?"

"Yep," Donald said. "It should be nothing now."

They climbed easily on to the top. It looked as though it might be clouding up in the west, so they hurried on down the cable route to camp.

Gregory awoke at dawn the next morning and took an hour's run. The other two had breakfast ready when he returned. They ate mostly in silence, not discussing the climb. It was too close.

"Well," Gregory said after they had finished eating, "I think it's time I got back to work"

Donald started laughing and Gregory joined in and then all three of them were laughing nearly hysterically.

"My stomach hurts," Donald gasped.

Gregory packed up and hiked down to the trailhead. He caught the bus to Denver, phoned Elizabeth to pick him up, and flew back to Minneapolis on a night flight. He had slept on the plane and saw no reason not to go to work, so he showered, shaved, and dressed for the office.

He had not shaved for the three weeks he had been gone. His beard, to his amazement, had not come in the salt and pepper grey that his hair was turning, but rather was as solid and brilliantly black as his hair had been in his youth. So when he shaved, he left a black moustache that was already becoming bushy.

"I like it," Elizabeth giggled when he came down for breakfast.

"I love you," Gregory said, reaching for her hand.

"Well, you sure stayed away long enough," Elizabeth said sourly, her thoughts shifting.

Gregory drove to the office and stopped in to tell Johanson he was back.

"Good to see you," Johanson said with a big smile. He stared at Gregory's new moustache, but said nothing about it. Then his face took on an expression of concern. "Everything all right, I hope, with the boy . . ."

"Yes," Gregory said, "fine."

"Fine!" Johanson beamed, "Glad you're back."

Gregory went back to work.

That night while undressing for bed, Gregory still had said nothing about the first thing he had noticed when he had gone into his and Elizabeth's bedroom that morning. The large old double bed was gone, and in its place were new twin beds separated by a night table. Now Gregory sat on his and looked across at the other.

Elizabeth was embarrassed.

"Well," she said, "now that Donnie and Connie are gone, I'm going to sleep late. And you get up so early that you'd wake me."

Gregory continued to say nothing.

Suddenly Elizabeth turned on him. "And it's not that we screw all that much anymore, either." She flipped off the light and crawled into her bed.

Elizabeth was almost never crude, even when drunk. Gregory lay back and thought about it. There had been a resurgence of love-making for almost two years when he first started running. Then he started his diets, and he began noticing how fat Elizabeth was getting. It was not that he had lost interest in sex. And only a couple of months ago (it seemed like years) they had made love a lot on the cruise.

But she was right if she meant that he did not care much. And she had gotten good beds. Gregory stretched out, luxuriating. He preferred sleeping alone now. He rolled over onto his stomach, spread out his arms, and went to sleep.

8

When Gregory settled down to work he discovered that even more of the major accounts he had handled for years had remained with Brown. Their place was taken by routine work that any beginner could have done. Gregory waited a week to make sure, then he made a list.

Johanson looked up, but the jovial expression that began to form on his face got only halfway there.

"I want to know what's going on," Gregory said, ignoring Johanson's hands that were fluttering at him to sit down.

"Well, I don't know," Johanson said. "I mean, what do you mean?"

"You know what I mean," Gregory said, tossing the list down on Johanson's desk.

Johanson picked up the piece of paper eagerly, relieved to fill his hands.

Gregory sat down, then scooted the chair around to face Johanson more squarely.

"I've handled some of those accounts for nearly twenty years. I want them back."

"But we thought . . ." Johanson began again.

"Never mind what you thought," Gregory said. "I've done important work in this office for a long time, and I don't intend to do flunky work now."

Johanson turned away from Gregory. He was spiraling the list.

"Now are you going to get those accounts for me, or do I have to go out and ask Buster Brown for them myself?"

Johanson spoke stubbornly. "We thought, that is some of us thought . . . I was puzzled, myself, but some of us thought you might be losing your . . . interest. You didn't seem to mind about the vice-presidency . . ."

"No," Gregory filled the pause. "I don't care about the vice-presidency. It would have been nice and I think I've earned it. Be that as it may, I've been doing important work in this office and I intend to continue doing important work."

"You don't talk shop much anymore," Johanson struggled on. This time Gregory let him hang.

"It was even suggested that you be eased . . ." Johanson glanced at Gregory and then turned quickly away again.

"I know that, Joe," Gregory said, unrelenting. "That's just absurd, and you know it."

Johanson swiveled around to face Gregory again. He took a neatly folded white handkerchief from his pocket and patted the sweat on his brow.

"Well, I did think it extreme," Johanson tried to smile. He looked at Gregory thoughtfully, hardness returning. His face took on a relaxed expression, the first time in months that he had seemed normal, Gregory thought.

"Of course you're right," Johanson said firmly. "Greg, I'm most appreciative that you brought it up. I'm damned glad this thing is settled." Johanson stood up, his big frame incongruous in his neat suiting. It was an artificial fabric of some greenish color that had a sheen in the light. He walked around and took Gregory by the shoulder, shook his hand. "Welcome back," he said. "I must say I'm glad."

"The accounts?"

"Give the boy a few days. I'll see to it. They'll all be back to you by next Monday."

Gregory eased to the door, but Johanson still held him. He had begun to look pained again.

"Greg, about the vice-presidency..."

"Joe," Gregory said, "I really don't care. Once I wanted it, but the boys are right to the extent that I don't seem to care so much about it anymore. I don't need to sit on the board. I can do important work for you here without being a vice-president. Just because I'm not concerned to join the management doesn't mean that I've forgotten how to do this job, or that I won't do it conscientiously, or ... Joe ... that I don't like the job. Joe, I do like the job. I intend to go on doing it, and liking it."

"Fine," Johanson said, releasing him. "Fine. I'm really glad of it, Greg. It's a great relief to me. I was getting pressure ..."

Gregory went out the door. Johanson was staring through the cage made by having pressed all the fingers of his big hands together.

Johanson did not wait until Monday. By the end of the next day, Gregory's job was reconstituted as it had been before he went on the cruise.

9

The following spring Gregory started exploring the neighborhood on his evening runs. He had enjoyed the surprises of exploring in Colorado, and he no longer cared about distance. As for speed, he could run around the lake a couple of times at eight minutes a mile, but any attempt to go a few seconds faster taxed him more than he thought it was worth. So he set out to run for an hour, often exceeded it, and sometimes ran two hours at a stretch.

On the weekends he sometimes ran morning and afternoon as he had in Colorado. He ventured out in straight lines as far as ten miles from home. Once on a Sunday he ran to the office, about eight miles. He went over to the little park, had a drink of water, and sat on his lunch bench for awhile. There were some joggers running around who nodded at him.

He thought about running to work and back every day. He grinned. Johanson would never accept it. He could imagine the conversation.

"What can I do for you, Greg, my boy?"

"Well, Joe, I wonder if you could get a shower and a locker installed in the Men's Room"

"In the Men's Room! Whatever for?"

"You see, Joe, I'm a runner, and I want to run to work. And I get a bit sweaty, so I'd need a shower when I got here."

Beads of sweat were forming on Johanson's imaginary brow, and Gregory hunched on the bench in delight. He was not going to let Johanson mop his brow.

"But you'd be wearing shorts."

"Yes."

"And you'd take a shower in the Men's Room . . . naked."

"Yes, I would."

"Out of the question! Utterly out of the question! We can't have a naked man in the Men's Room. What if someone came in?"

Gregory was relentless.

"But Joe, a lot of men run to work."

"Who?"

"Well, there's Senator Proxmire, he runs to work in Washington."

"What!" Gregory made Johanson's hands stand up in horror. "That fairy? Why I heard he had hair transplants on his head."

Gregory wiped Johanson's bald brow with Johanson's big hands.

Well, he would not want to use up his running time that way. It might be nice to run around the little park during the noon hour, like Fred and Gene. Johanson might tolerate that if he did not have to discuss it. But Gregory was happy enough that only a few people at the office knew he ran at all, and none of them knew how much.

On his rambles, Gregory ran past the high school track several times. Had the twins still been in school he would not have run near the high school, but one afternoon in early fall he turned in and circled the track.

It was a quarter of a mile, and he had never run on cinders before. The even, springy surface felt good, so Gregory speeded up the second lap.

"Hi there, old man."

Gregory nodded curtly. He had learned to contend with—if

not to tolerate—the talky pick-up jogger who ran on the open streets. This was a smart high school kid.

"Thought I'd get in shape before the cross-country season starts," the kid said. He was loping along easily, talking normally.

Gregory was breathing heavily, but he did not want to slow down with the kid beside him.

The kid was humming. "Say, how long you been running?"

"About thirty minutes," Gregory said.

"No, no," the kid laughed, "I mean do you run regular?"

"Yes."

"How often?"

"Every day."

"How long?"

Gregory thought for a moment. "Almost six years."

The kid moved over to look at Gregory as he ran.

"Well, your form's not bad. You move your arms too much, but almost everyone does. Is that as fast as you go?"

Gregory nodded. They came around the curve, and the kid said, "Stop."

Gregory stopped reluctantly, he seldom stopped on his runs.

"Do you want to run faster?"

"Yes," Gregory said slowly. "Yes, I've tried, but I don't seem to get faster."

"Do you run intervals?"

"What?" Gregory said.

"You've got to run intervals or you'll never get faster. Look, you feel ok now, don't you? I mean, you aren't worn out?"

"I often run a couple of hours," Gregory said.

"Good," the kid said. "Long slow distance, that's good for endurance, and you've got to do it for the long races. But if you want to run faster, you've got to do intervals." He looked at Gregory's puzzled face and went on. "Here's what we'll do. We'll run the quarter. Four times, with a minute's rest between each interval. Got it? Thirty seconds would be better, but it's your first time. Now I'll set a pace and you keep up. Ok? Now we've got to go, remember, you got to push it if it's going to do any good. Ready?"

"Go!"

Gregory plunged after the boy. He ran as hard as he could, but was always half a step behind. They coasted to a stop where they had started.

"One-thousand-one, one-thousand-two, . . ." the boy counted as Gregory caught his breath.

"Go!"

They ran around the track again. Gregory's knees were beginning to feel weak.

"Go!"

Gregory could not keep up, but the boy urged him on. The crazy kid wants to be a coach, Gregory thought.

"Go!"

Gregory snapped up. He had bent over and had not caught his breath. It was the last time. Gregory tried, but he had had it.

"Come on!" the kid yelled, "You can do it. Give!"

Gregory ran. His breath was gone. His chest burned, but still the boy kept just half a step ahead, kept yelling at him. Yelling! Gregory could hardly breathe, and this kid was running along ahead of him yelling at him.

"Come on now, get ready, we're going to sprint the last hundred yards. Come on! Forget what you've done before. Now. Run!"

Gregory flung himself after the boy. He did not know what he was running on, he knew he had no strength left. He forced his feet off the ground, he willed his legs to swing, he could not breathe.

When he finished the fourth interval, Gregory went over onto his hands and knees on the grass inside the track. He had to breathe, but he could not. He wanted to throw up, but there was only dry retching.

The boy stood beside him until Gregory had recovered slightly, then reached a hand under his arm to lift him up. "That was great, pops," he said. "I knew you could do it."

Gregory was resisting, but the kid was insistent.

"Best to walk around afterwards," the kid said.

He guided Gregory out onto the track and they walked around a lap, the kid talking the whole time.

"How old are you? Forty-six? Yeah, I'd have said about that. Well, you could go a lot faster. Men over sixty could beat you now. But you've got what it takes. You can see that. You've just got to run intervals. You got a stopwatch? No? Well, get yourself one. Time your intervals. Work them down. You'll be amazed at how you can improve. There's no other way."

When they finished the lap the kid said, "Well, I've got to take off. Keep at it. You did great."

Gregory nodded, and then, after the boy had run off, too late, Gregory said, "Thanks."

Gregory jogged home. It was a short run for him, but he was sore. Now he understood. There was another door. He had opened the first one, and just stepped a short distance inside, that first time he had run around the lake. The pain and breathless agony he had felt then, the muscle aches, they were the entrance fee. But he had not paid much. Still, he had paid.

Now he would have to pay again, if he wanted to go on, if he wanted to go through this second door that had opened just a crack for him. And this was a stiffer fee. Intervals were hard. And you pressed them always, the boy had said that. What had he said? You had to get breathless. Gregory had been doing aerobic running. He never ran fast enough to hurt. He ran at speeds at which he could take in enough oxygen to burn up the poisons that were forming in his muscles. So he did not hurt. But to increase his speed, and his long-run endurance, he would have to do anaerobic running. That was what the intervals were for. It was not doing any good unless he ended breathless and in pain. The chest pains were from the body's attempt to take in more oxygen to burn up the poisons that were causing the muscle pain. He had to increase his tolerance of the pain to go faster, and in doing so his lungs would increase their oxygen capacity so he could go faster to increase his pain to increase his tolerance to go faster to increase his pain to go faster . . .

The next day Gregory bought a stop watch. He did four intervals at the beginning of his run, but they spoiled the rest of it. Thereafter he designed his routes to finish at the track. He would do four intervals, then trot home.

The door was beginning to open wider. He would get through. And then? Gregory came up short. There were other doors beyond.

During the winter the track was often full of snow and it was not easy to run intervals. So Gregory started simply varying the pace on his long runs through the streets and around the lake. He would run as hard as he could for a few blocks, jog, then run a middling speed as he felt like it. It was a good winter with lots of snow. Some of Gregory's best days were in bright sunshine through the plowed streets, snow standing high on the curbs. Some days he would return home with his moustache caked solid with ice.

When spring came he started doing intervals regularly on the track again. One day the boy appeared and ran the set with him. Gregory was pleased to notice that it was not quite so easy for his coach to breathe as it had been the first time.

"You're really improving," the boy panted. "Now you ought to start putting them together."

"What?"

"Do halves, now. Run four half-miles. Work up until you can do four one-mile intervals at your top speed. Then you're on your way."

Doors . . .

Gregory tried doing halves the next evening. It was not easy.

He repeated to himself mindlessly as he ran around, "Nobody said it was easy."

Gregory worked hard all summer. By fall he could run four interval miles at six and a half minutes a mile, with one minute rest between each. He knew, of course, what was next.

He tried it all at once, with the goal of doing four miles in twenty-eight minutes or less. The first three miles he did not look at the stop watch. By now he could estimate his pace fairly well, and it felt as though he were doing at least seven minutes a mile. At the end of three miles he glanced at the watch. He was twenty seconds down, but if he increased his speed for the last mile, he could just make it.

Gregory strained forward. He ran three quarters, then looked at the watch just before the last lap. He would have to sprint the last quarter if he were to make it.

Gregory went all out. As he crossed the line he pressed the button on the stop watch. He jogged on, slowing down. It had hurt, but he was used to that now. And he had not been out to do everything he could, he just wanted to put together four seven-minute miles. He glanced at the watch. Twenty-seven minutes, fifty-two seconds.

Gregory's face burst into a grin. He jogged on around and then ran home and on around the lake once, playing at running fast and running slow. Two weeks later he ran four miles in twenty-six minutes. He had put those four six-and-a-half-minute miles together.

It was a very late fall, and although Gregory kept up his speed work, he loved more the long runs through the tree-lined streets, through the parks, around the little lakes here and there. Sometimes he drove to the university campus to run on the track there. He wondered that he had not found running when he was in college. But he was too worldly-wise then, a returned veteran, beer drinker with a car, hot for Elizabeth, and set on security, a home, and a good job. He would have scorned running then. Now he ran across open areas on the farm campus. He ran for many miles along the river.

One day he was running along some unfamiliar streets, peering down each side street trying to figure out where he had left his car. He looked down one street and turned forward, but suddenly did a double-take, looking back down the side street quickly with the thought that it was the right one to take after all.

As Gregory twisted his neck to the right again, he came down on his right heel with all his weight.

It felt like lightening. It entered Gregory's body just above his right buttock, just to the side of the base of his spinal column. It traveled diagonally about three inches to the base of his spine where it ripped out of his body and was gone.

Gregory stopped instantly, bent over with pain. He straightened up part way. He could feel where the spasm had been. His face was white and he was sweating all over. He shuffled his right leg forward and tried to put his weight on it.

It was there again.

The pain nauseated him. The best thing to do, though, was to keep moving. He could, in fact, move everything despite the pain, so it was probably only a muscle spasm. But he had better keep moving before it stiffened up.

It was a mile and a half back to the car. Gregory took five minutes to get into the driver's seat. The pain was excruciating. He drove as much as he could with his left foot.

At home he was not sure he could get out of the car. Finally he did. Elizabeth was not in the kitchen. She caught Gregory crawling up the stairs.

"Hurt my back."

Elizabeth helped him undress. He could not reach down to untie his shoes.

"No, no, don't touch me," Gregory raised his voice.

Elizabeth stood back while Gregory rolled into the tub.

He began to relax tentatively in the hot water, but the ache was unbelievable.

"I'm going to call the doctor," Elizabeth said.

"No, let's wait until tomorrow. I don't think anything is broken. It's probably just muscular."

"You may have slipped a disk."

Gregory had considered that. "I don't think so. I couldn't have walked all that way then. I don't feel any pain anywhere else, it isn't like a pinched nerve or anything, I think. I can move my toes and foot ok. It's all there in my lower back." Gregory smiled weakly. A man with a lower back pain.

Elizabeth looked grim, but agreed.

Gregory soaked for an hour. He felt somewhat better, and although the pain and the hot water had weakened him considerably, he did not have too much trouble drying himself and getting into bed. He was grateful that he had his own bed so Elizabeth's presence and movements would not make him tense. His every move was slow, and careful, and painful.

Elizabeth brought their dinner up to the bedroom on trays. Gregory propped himself up gingerly with pillows, but he could tolerate no weight on his right buttock. As soon as he finished eating he slid down flat on his back.

He read awhile, trying to get away from the discomfort. Elizabeth watched television. The evening dragged on. Elizabeth went downstairs to make popcorn. Gregory ate a little, and even accepted a beer.

Then he had to go to the bathroom. As he shifted his legs to the side of the bed, an electric shock went through his back again. Cold sweat popped out on Gregory's body.

"You're going to have to get me a bottle or something," Gregory said.

Elizabeth went away and came back with a quart fruit jar. After careful maneuvering, Gregory got positioned over the jar. Nothing happened for awhile, but eventually he managed to relieve himself. Elizabeth took the jar into the bathroom and brought it back rinsed.

"I can't reach it on the floor," Gregory said.

Elizabeth put the jar on the night table. At midnight she turned off the television.

"You want anything more?"

"No."

Elizabeth snapped off the light.

Gregory could not go to sleep on his back. He had drawn up his knees, which eased the pain some, but this made it even more impossible for him to sleep. Lying on his stomach was out of the question. He straightened out. He moved eventually over onto his right side. The next morning he woke up lying on his stomach, his back aching intolerably.

The pain was so intense when he tried to move that he moaned; evidently he had to if he were to move at all.

Elizabeth woke up. She watched, and then said, "I'm going to call the doctor."

"Well, not for a couple of hours," Gregory said, "he won't be there."

Elizabeth dressed and went downstairs to prepare breakfast. Gregory had managed to roll onto his back, but he could not sit up. He moved up fractions of an inch, and got back onto his stomach although the slight sag of the bed increased the pain in his back. He slid slowly to the side of the bed and eased his left leg off onto the floor. He remained that way, half upright, until Elizabeth returned, and he ate some breakfast in that position. He used his bottle. Then he resumed his attempt to get out of bed.

"Don't do that," Elizabeth said. She took the breakfast trays downstairs.

Overall, it took Gregory about an hour to get upright. Then he could put no weight on his right leg. Elizabeth brought him a pair of crutches left over from Donald's skiing accident. Gregory swung his way into the bathroom and positioned himself over the stool. The bowel movement was a long time coming, but Gregory persisted, determined to demonstrate that there were no complicated disruptions down there.

He walked around with the crutches, and by ten o'clock, when Elizabeth got the doctor on the phone, Gregory could walk without the crutches by putting weight very gingerly on his right foot.

Gregory had objected when Elizabeth had the phone installed in the bedroom, but she had argued that it was not his worry, it was over by her bed. He took it now to tell the doctor briefly what his problem was.

"There's not much we can do about lower back pain," the doctor said. "I can give you something for the pain."

"No, I don't need that," Gregory said.

"You can come in for an x-ray, but I doubt that it would show anything. Like you say, if it were a ruptured disk or something in the vertebrae, you probably wouldn't be moving around like you are. Stay off it. Soak it in hot baths, and use a heating pad. Sleep on a hard surface, put a board under the mattress or just sleep on the floor. And sleep on your back. If it doesn't get better in a week or so, come in and we'll x-ray it."

Gregory managed to sit in a chair for dinner, but he did not try to go downstairs.

"I can't sleep in that bed," Gregory said. He decided he could not sleep on the floor in their bedroom, either. There had not been much space before, and now with twin beds and night tables there was even less.

Gregory went into Donald's room and took the ensolite pad he had slept on in Colorado out of the closet. It was full length and comfortable enough despite being only three-eighths of an inch thick. Gregory laid it on the floor. Elizabeth put down sheets and blankets.

"Good," she said, "you won't wake me up with your groaning now."

Gregory thought she was joking, but she had not smiled. He eased himself into a chair to read, not going with Elizabeth back into their bedroom to watch television. About ten o'clock she brought him popcorn and beer. He ate the popcorn, but left the beer. He had not been drinking it for so long that it had not sat well the night before. This reminded him of the jar. His muscles had congealed again, but he struggled up. He moved about the room for awhile, supporting himself on the bed, the dresser, and the walls until he could walk into the other bedroom to get his jar.

"How do you feel?" Elizabeth glanced at him.

"All right," Gregory said.

He had missed two days of work, Thursday and Friday, then the weekend passed. He got up at six Monday morning, and by eight he decided he could go to work. However, he did not think he could drive, so Elizabeth took him. For the first time since his charley horse, Gregory took the elevator instead of walking up the stairs to the office.

He walked very carefully to avoid comment, but several people noticed. Gregory learned that half his co-workers had lower back trouble. He heard about a variety of cures, none of which seemed to alleviate the problem.

At five, after he had been in the car a few minutes, Gregory said, "This isn't the way home."

"I called the doctor," Elizabeth said. "He said you could come in for an x-ray now, and he'd see you tomorrow."

Gregory was holding himself up off the car seat with his arms. He supposed it would do no harm to be sure.

"How'd you say you did this?" the doctor asked the next morning when Gregory went in to see him. "The x-rays, by the way, showed nothing unusual, as I'd expected."

"I was running," Gregory said.

"Yes, well it's often some unusual exertion like that that does it."

"But I run a lot," Gregory said, annoyed.

"You mean you're a jogger?"

Gregory nodded, although it further annoyed him to be called a jogger.

Now the doctor looked annoyed. "It's not good for you," he said firmly. "A man your age. If you knew how many men come in here with bad knees and backs from jogging. And heart attacks! They say it's good for the heart. I say it's damned foolishness! A man your age has no business running around like a silly adolescent."

Gregory saw the look of agreement on Elizabeth's face.

"Now you rest that back as much as possible," the doctor said sternly. "No more running. You aren't getting any younger, and you'll just have to face up to it and learn to take care of yourself. Fifty percent of American men have this lower back problem, and you're one of them. There's not a damned thing we can do about it, so get used to it. I could give you some exercises to do when you get better, but you won't do them, so I won't. I don't know that they do any good anyway. Cut down on your activities. Don't lift things. And *don't run*."

Gregory was furious as he left the doctor's office. He sat in the car looking at Elizabeth until she said, "I think the doctor's absolutely right. You're too old for that silliness. You ought to know it yourself by now. Look how you hurt yourself with that running."

Gregory turned and looked out the window. Just at that moment they passed two middle-aged joggers. They had on new warm-up suits, and were overweight. Gregory turned again to look straight down the road.

He tried to learn to sleep on his back. He could eventually fall asleep that way, but it took a long time. He lay awake late every night, thinking.

He improved very slowly. After two weeks he tried Donald's bed, but it was much too soft. Gregory lay down on the pad on the floor again.

A month passed, and Gregory still had to be very careful how he walked. Fellow sufferers at the office told him it might take six months to clear up, then he was likely to have another attack. Once it hits you, it never leaves you, they said.

Running was out of the question, but Gregory started taking short walks during the noon hour. One day he stood watching Fred and Gene run around the little park. It was about a quarter mile circuit. The winter day was bright and crisp. Six minutes a mile, Gregory thought, they must be going six minutes a mile.

Gregory had started toward the office when he made a sudden decision, turned back, and hurried as best he could toward the office building where Fred and Gene worked. When they came back, he held the door open, and without preliminaaries he started telling them about his back problem. He told how he had worked up to running six and half minutes a mile for four miles, that he had been running at least eight miles a day almost every day for two or three years, and probably as much as twenty miles two or three times a month.

"I don't want to stop running. What do I do?"

The two runners had listened without comment. Fred had made noises encouraging Gregory to go on, but that was all.

When Gregory was finished, Fred asked, "What kind of shoes do you wear?"

The question embarrassed Gregory. When his fancy Nikes had worn down badly within a year, he had returned to THE ATHLETE'S FOOT. It was now OMNI SPORTS, with a doubled floor space. The stark unity and bold colors of the running gear were now gone, replaced by a diversity of equipment of all sorts. Along one wall were guns and fishing tackle. There were kids' football outfits, and in the back were skis and camping equipment. The running shoes were in the same corner, but the selection had diminished. And the smart young clerk did not know what he was talking about. Gregory had to show him the LD-1000s in the Nike catalog.

"Oh, those are too expensive, we wouldn't stock them. Let's try these." The clerk brought out a heavy pair of Adidas that were obviously made for casual sports wear, not for running. "We sell more of this style than any other shoe in the store," the clerk said, lacing the shoe up firmly.

Gregory stood up, but the open route around the shop for trying out shoes had long been closed by displays.

"Do you have Converse All Stars?" Gregory asked, sitting down.

"Sure," the clerk said. He got a pair.

They were very much as Gregory remembered them from high school. Low-cut canvas tennis shoes, with rubber toes. They were not Nikes, but they felt all right, and at $14 a pair, they were only a third the price of the Nikes.

As Gregory got out his Master Charge, he said, "Say, I think I'll take two pairs." He often got his shoes soaked, and it would be good to have a pair to shift to.

The Converse All Stars wore out fairly rapidly, but they were cheap, and he often wore the heels completely down before discarding them. He got some pleasure in wearing them out completely.

But they were not really running shoes.

"Well," Gregory said to Fred now, "I haven't been wearing real running shoes. I've been wearing Converse All Stars, you know, tennis shoes."

"Do you wear the heels down?"

"Yes, I do."

Fred glanced at Gene, who had not rushed off this time. "That's probably it, isn't it?"

"Jesus," Gene said, "Converse All Stars?" He turned to Gregory. "You really run six-and-a-half in them?"

Gregory nodded.

"Jesus," Gene said.

"That's probably it," Fred said. "Look, you wear down the heels and your foot comes down wrong. Guys have got back trouble from only a quarter of an inch worn off. You've really got to be careful. And anyway, those tennis shoes don't give you enough support. And your heel comes down hard, you know."

"I'll get new shoes," Gregory said. "When I first started I had Nike LD-1000s, but they seemed so expensive."

"Well worth it," Gene put in.

"Yes, get good shoes," Fred said. "But that's not going to do it all. What about exercises?"

"I do some."

"What?"

"Well, I don't do that one you showed me. I mean, I got over the charley horse. What I do is touching my toes and deep knee bends, sit-ups and pushups, before I run." He did not always do them. They were too boring.

"The sit-ups and pushups are ok," Fred said, "but you should never do jerky toe-touching, and the deep knee bends will kill your knees." Fred scrabbled around in the top of his locker and pulled out a small booklet. "The worn shoes probably brought it on," he said, "but the real problem is that runners build muscles up unevenly. Your calves and the backs of your thighs get stronger, so the fronts of your thighs and your stomach muscles get relatively weaker. Here," he handed the booklet to Gregory. It was titled *Exercises for Runners*.

"Now your back. It says in there that all these muscles get shorter as they get stronger. And you might think that touching your toes would stretch them out, but in fact jerky exercises like that cause a rebound that actually shortens the muscles. So everything you do has led to your back problem—the uneven shoes, the weak stomach muscles, and the short back muscles. You get a twist or a jolt or bad stretch, and bingo, you get a muscle spasm in your lower back."

Gregory looked at the booklet.

"Take it home, you can borrow it. I've memorized it, anyway. You should do stretching exercises for at least ten minutes everytime before you run, more if possible. Some people do stretching exercises for an hour a day. It really pays off."

"But do you know anyone who has as bad a back as I do?"

"Sure I've known a couple."

"But did they get over it? The doctor said . . ."

"Doctors, schmoctors!" Gene burst in. "What they know about it you could shove up your nose."

"What did the doctor say?" Fred asked.

"Well, he said I'd always have a bad back, and to quit running."

"Bull!" Gene exclaimed.

"He just doesn't know what he's talking about," Fred said. "Most doctors don't know anything at all about running. You'll be ok if you do these exercises and wear decent shoes. I've known people in as bad a shape as you, and they aren't bothered at all, now they're watching it. You'll be ok."

"Six-and-a-half is good for a man your age," Gene said.

"He said I was too old for running."

Gene just snorted this time.

"You know," Fred said, clapping him on the shoulder, "how old are you? Forty-six, you know, there's a guy in the Twin City Track Club who is fifty-five, and he can almost beat me. And there are runners in their seventies who can run you into the ground. Don't pay any attention to those doctors. Or go to one who runs himself. Say, we've got to get back to work."

Gregory shuffled back to the office and put the booklet into his briefcase. Elizabeth had not liked to get up to take him to work, so he was driving the car himself again, although it felt bad for him. He drove home, went up to Donald's room, and took out the booklet.

Yoga! But that's for kooks, Gregory thought, as he fidgeted in the chair. He read the booklet through rapidly, and then read it through again. All the writer claimed for yoga was that it stretched your muscles. And the reasons why runners should stretch their muscles were incontrovertible. Gregory had no doubts now as to how and why he had hurt his back. How could the doctor say that it just happened? Or that there was nothing you could do about it?

Gregory stood up, locked his knees straight, and bent over slowly. His fingers reached his knees before he decided the pain was enough. He glanced at his watch and held that position for three minutes, long enough to relax in it. He straightened up slowly. Maybe it helped a little.

He tried some of the other exercises that were not likely to strain his back. Then he sat down at Donald's desk and wrote out a check to send to World Publications—the address was on the booklet—for a copy.

Gregory's copy of *Exercises for Runners* came a week later. He returned Fred's copy, which by then he, too, had almost memorized.

Along with the booklet came *The Complete Runner's Catalog*. Gregory read it all the way through, and then made out an order. First, booklets. He ordered,

> *Dr. Sheehan on Running*
> *Runner's Training Guide*
> *Run Gently, Run Long*
> *The Runner's Diet Guide to Distance Running*
> *Age of the Runner*
> *Athletes' Feet*
> *The Long Run Solution*
> *Running After Forty*
> *The Running Body*
> *Running With Style*
> *Step Up to Racing*
> *The Running Foot Doctor*
> *Van Aaken Method*
> *Jog, Run, Race*
> *Tale of the Ancient Marathoner*

He also ordered two new pairs of Nike LD-1000s, a Sole Repair Kit with a pack of 100 glue pellets, extra shoe laces, six pairs of socks, a Nike Tote Bag, and a new visor. He decided he did not need new shorts or T-shirts or warm-up suits.

The total order, with postage, came to just over $170. Gregory stared at the figure for a moment, then wrote out the check. He started to seal the envelope, but then took the order out and changed his home address to his office address.

When the order came, Gregory put the running equipment in the bottom of his file cabinet—he was not up to running again yet—and took the booklets home. He had boxed up most of Donald's things and put them in the closet. The bookshelves above Donald's desk now contained a batch of Gregory's paperbound mysteries and adventure books. He put the running booklets on a shelf by themselves, but they fell over. Gregory went downstairs to the bookshelves he had built on either side of the fireplace. Most of the books were from Elizabeth's periodic memberships in the Book-of-the-Month Club. She seldom remembered to return the form, so they had a batch of books no one had read.

Gregory started looking through the books. Half an hour later he took an armload—all that interested him—upstairs to put on Donald's bookshelf to support the running booklets.

After dinner, Gregory started in on the booklets. Why had he not read about running before? Well, there was no question but that he could run again. And this time he would do it right.

The crankiest booklet of the lot—in a batch that was at least half inspirational rather than informative literature—was *The Runner's Diet*. Gregory read of runners who lived mostly on raw potatoes, who ran Marathons after fasting for seven days, and who advocated strict vegetarianism. Carbohydrate loading, in which you eat no carbohydrates for three days, then gorge on them the next three days during which your starved body overreacts to store more energy in the muscles than normal, and then you race the seventh day utilizing this increased store—that seemed well-supported. Gregory decided to try it later.

Gregory was always drawn to weight charts. Now he found a formula he could really get his teeth into. To get the average weight of an American male, you allow 110 pounds for his first five feet of height, and five and a half pounds for each inch above that. At five-eight, Gregory, if average, would weigh 154. He remembered quite well that this was the weight recommended on the pamphlet—he still had it—the urologist had given him. He had felt smug about getting down to 150.

However, Gregory read, Dr. Sheehan says that the average American weight is that of a race of slobs, and has no relation to health. The healthiest weight is ten percent less than the average. So according to Dr. Sheehan, Gregory should weigh 138.6 pounds, say 139. And if that were not sobering enough, Dr. Van Aaken says that the best weight for a runner—and the healthiest for anyone, for that matter—is twenty percent less than average. For Gregory, that would be 123.2 pounds. That seemed absurd.

Gregory went into the bathroom and got out the scales. Elizabeth never used them, anyway. He put them in the corner of Donald's room, took off his clothes, and weighed himself. He was back up to 165, fifteen pounds heavier than the low of 150 a couple of years ago.

Gregory stepped off, then stepped up on the scales again. Too much.

If anything was reasonable in the booklets he was reading, it was the repeated statement that extra weight means more work for a runner and slows him down. It also contributes to the sorts of shock injury from which Gregory was suffering.

If he could not run yet, at least he could prepare by getting his weight down. Elizabeth did not like him to diet, and always sabotaged him by preparing a lot of good food and pressing it on him. Perhaps this time she would accept the argument that it would be good for his back if he cut his weight down.

Gregory knew that he could lose weight, but this time he wanted to maintain the loss. The writers of the running booklets advocated low weight, but they did not say much about how to maintain it. So Gregory stopped at Dalton's Book Store on the way home from work one evening, to see what was available.

The selection was enormous. Every major health nut in America had written at least one book. Some of them had written half a dozen. Gregory browsed for an hour. He rejected all books stressing one food (only grapefruit and cottage cheese, or only meat), those based on Oriental religious practices, and those on fasting. He finally settled on three books,

Sugar Blues
The Thin Book by a Formerly Fat Psychiatrist
Dr. Siegal's Natural Fiber Permanent Weight-Loss Diet

The book by the psychiatrist was funny. Anyway, Gregory thought he had the will power if he set his mind to it.

What fascinated Gregory was the history of refined sugar and white flour, whose use had totally altered man's diet in the last 100 years. By the time Gregory had finished the books on sugar and fiber, he was convinced that diabetes and hypoglycemia, ulcers and diverticulitis, and depression and hemorrhoids were in some large part often worsened, if not directly caused by diets high in sugar and low in fiber. Not only that, although he had put aside books on natural foods he was now convinced that he ought to avoid as many processed foods as possible. Almost all of them contain sugar and flour that provide naked carbohydrates—they simply lay on fat without providing any vitamins or minerals.

When Gregory tried to explain this to Elizabeth, she laughed and laughed. He argued that he did not mean that sugar and flour caused these diseases directly, they just led to a diet that brought them on. He got quite heated about it, telling Elizabeth that she did not know what she was talking about, and that she ought to read the books herself.

"Fat chance!" Elizabeth said, and began laughing again so hard that she had to sit down. Gregory could not keep from laughing himself. But he was still convinced.

Gregory read about how hard it is to avoid sugar. Yes, he would have thought about toothpaste, sugar in toothpaste ... Well, there are a few brands without. He knew it was in breakfast food, but up to sixty percent? Would he have to give up Wheaties again? And now that he thought about it he realized that there had to be sugar in ham, and in some other processed meats. Where would you be least likely to look for hidden sugar? Gregory laughed out loud when he read the answer. Salt! Good old free-flowing salt. It has sugar in it to help it flow free.

Gregory visited several health nut stores before he found one that actually sold food rather than being packed with thousands of white plastic bottles full of pills and tea made from alfalfa. In the Nitty Gritty, he bought brown rice, whole wheat flour, rye flour, bran, rolled oats, and yogurt. He bought half a pound of peaches and some carrots raised without fertilizer and pesticides, but decided at once that the much cheaper vegetables and fruits at the supermarket were natural enough for him.

Elizabeth made some wisecracks, but she tried his bran muffins and pronounced them excellent.

"Put lots of raisins in the next batch, hey?"

"Ok," Gregory said. Apparently Elizabeth would not oppose his cooking.

Gregory began to prepare vegetable casseroles. Elizabeth pitched in and ate as much as he did. After a few weeks Gregory lost any great desire for meat, so Elizabeth would often supplement her meal with steak. And to fruit for desert, she added pastries and ice cream. Elizabeth complimented Gregory's cooking from the beginning. She was not just tired of cooking. Gregory could tell that she genuinely liked the food he prepared.

He had decided on a 1200 calorie diet. When he ate out, he kept track, and ate less the next day to maintain the average. After two months, he was down to 145, a loss of twenty pounds. And then—it had been five months since his injury—he thought he could start running, very cautiously, again. So he raised his intake to 1600 calories a day with the hope that he would have enough strength for running and still lose weight slowly. He had set himself the somewhat arbitrary goal of 140 pounds. It was about what Dr. Sheehan recommended, but was still seventeen pounds heavier than the mad Dr. Van Aaken advised. And maybe Gregory would not even reach 140. Van Aaken recommended 1600 calories as a weight maintenance diet, although other experts said that someone running as much as Gregory needed up to 2400. Gregory hoped that his caloric needs for weight maintenance were high.

He was hungry.

10

One evening while Elizabeth was watching television in their room—Gregory had moved the big color set up from downstairs for her—Gregory took a set of his running clothes downstairs and put them in the car. The next day at work he quit at eleven-thirty and put his clothes and a new pair of Nikes in his bag. He walked over to the office building where Fred and Gene worked. When he pushed open the door to the janitors' locker room, he saw that Fred and Gene were already dressing.

"I don't have anyplace over there," Gregory indicated with his head," and I wondered if I could dress here?"

"Sure," Fred said, "pick a locker."

"It'll be all right?"

"Don't know why not. Matter of fact, we never asked anybody. Just came in and put locks on a couple of unused lockers. Now everybody in the building thinks its our locker room. Here, shove your clothes in my locker today, and bring your own lock tomorrow." Fred and Gene went on out.

Gregory dressed, and laced up his new Nikes. They did feel good. He went outside, walked fifty yards, and then started jogging slowly. He was stiff. And his back ached, but it did not feel bad. It felt as though that aching was doing it good. Gregory jogged around four times, a mile, then he did some stretching exercises. He jogged around again and went back to the locker room to take a shower. One nice thing about a big building like this, he thought, was that there would be unlimited hot water.

"First time since the back, eh?" Fred said.

"Yes."

"Go ok?"

"Still aches, but seems ok."

"It'll be ok. Just take it easy."

It was a month before Gregory felt that his back was safe. He then began to speed up. He was sure that his lowered weight—he was now down to 140—allowed him to run faster. But he did not try to keep up with Fred and Gene.

After he had been running for two months, Gregory took his other pair of Nikes home. The noon run was not enough.

"Hunh-unh!" Elizabeth said when he came downstairs in his running clothes. She stared at the gaudy new shoes. "You're not going to start that again. You'll hurt yourself permanently."

"I've been doing exercises for my back, Elizabeth," Gregory said. "And I've been running during the noon hour at work for two months. I'm fine." Gregory went on out without arguing further. Elizabeth was watching at the door when he returned.

"What's for dinner?" she asked.

Gregory went upstairs, showered, then came down and prepared dinner.

Gregory had been doing some of his exercises on the ensolite pad he slept on, but it was not big enough and it slid around. One day he returned to OMNI SPORTS in the Northwest Plaza to see what they had. Nothing was suitable. They had some fold-up exercise mats of foam rubber, made for people who were not going to use them.

"Isn't there anything better?"

"This is all that's available," the clerk lied.

Gregory was exasperated. "Can I see the manager?"

The clerk bristled. "He's usually busy."

"See," Gregory said.

Gregory looked around the store for a few minutes.

"You wanted to see me?"

Gregory was not sure, but he thought this was the same fellow who had managed the old ATHLETE'S FOOT. If so, he had put on some weight. But he still looked pleasant and relaxed.

Gregory explained his problem.

"You want a regular module from a wrestling mat," the manager said, shifting his gum from one side of his mouth to the other. "Here, I'll show you."

They went into a tiny office where the manager searched through a pile of catalogs to find the one he wanted. He flipped it open to a page, bent it back, and showed Gregory.

It was a rectangle, six by six feet, meant to go together with others to make a large wrestling mat. An inch and a half thick, solid, with a heavy duty vinylite cover. Gregory glanced at the price. $96.

"That's it," the manager said. "Last a lifetime. I can special order it if you want."

Gregory wanted it. Where would he put it? He read the description over again. It seemed a little large, but it was exactly what he now wanted.

"All right," he said slowly. "Yes, order one for me." He was thinking rapidly. How would he get it home?

"Say," he said, "could you have it delivered to my home? I don't know how I'd get it there otherwise."

"Sure thing," the manager said, taking down Gregory's name and address on an order blank. "Cash or charge?"

Ten days later the mat arrived just as Gregory got home from work. He had dismantled Donald's bed and stored it in the basement. He gave the delivery man an extra five dollars to carry the mat upstairs. It dominated the corner of the room.

"What on earth?" Elizabeth said.

"When the delivery man had left, Elizabeth asked, "Are you going to sleep on that thing?"

Gregory stretched out on the mat. He guessed he had intended to sleep on it. He had stayed in Donald's room sleeping on the ensolite pad much longer than was necessary for his back, he supposed. Whenever he considered going back to his bed in the other room with Elizabeth, his thoughts slid away from it. He had grown used to the quiet of a private bedroom. In the master bedroom were the telephone, the television set, Elizabeth's smoking, Elizabeth. . .

"Because if you are, I wish you'd take down your bed in the other bedroom. There's little enough space for me to dress in there, anyway."

"All right," Gregory said. He got up and went into the other bedroom to do it right then. Elizabeth helped.

After they had stored the bed beside Donald's in the basement, Elizabeth said, "I've been thinking. Let's take our old double bed back up for me, and bring the other twin bed down. I never have liked that narrow twin bed, and it's too hard. I'd like to have the old double bed back in my bedroom."

They hauled the old bed up, dismantled the other twin bed, carried it down, and then installed the old one in Elizabeth's bedroom. Elizabeth fussed making it up, and praised it.

Gregory went into his bedroom now and began removing the remainder of Donald's paraphernalia. Gregory had left up some posters and knick-knacks as long as it was not his room, but now he removed everything and packed it in boxes. He cleaned out all the drawers and the closet, and began carrying Donald's stuff to the basement. While he was carrying, Elizabeth cleaned all his clothes out of the drawers and closet of their old joint bedroom—out of her bedroom—and put Gregory's belongings in his new bedroom.

It took them several hours, during which they had not thought of dinner.

"Let's go to that new Italian restaurant," Gregory said.

"Oh, yes, let me just change."

Gregory changed into a suit.

The lights were low and the food was excellent. They shared a bottle of wine, and sat long over dessert, coffee, and after-dinner liqueur. They spoke fondly to one another, about the twins—Constance was soon to be married, Donald was in graduate school—and about old times. It was after eleven when they got home.

"I'm tired," Elizabeth said. "I'm just going to turn in."

"Me, too," Gregory agreed.

"Night, night," Elizabeth said, kissing Gregory on the cheek. She suddenly erupted in a big laugh, ending with tears in her eyes.

"It's been quite a day, hasn't it?" she said.

"Yes," Gregory said, "it has. Good night."

The mat was an excellent bed.

11

Gregory had neglected calisthenics because he thought them a bore. Now, on his new mat, he began to take pleasure in the yoga-based stretching exercises. Soon he could bend over and hold his fingers on his toes for three minutes. He felt more limber than he ever had before.

Gregory went through his routine in the evenings. Elizabeth had made some apologetic remarks about the color television being in her bedroom, but Gregory waved them aside. He took the small bedside black and white set, telling her truthfully that it would be quite adequate. He watched the news, but not much else.

He liked being in his room alone. At first there was some awkwardness about his and Elizabeth's saying goodnight, but it became so apparent that if one walked in, the other viewed it as an intrusion—however slight—that they gave it up. Gregory solved the problem by saying good night when they went upstairs after dinner. They did not cross at the bathroom, for the master bedroom had its own, and Gregory used the one at the end of the hall.

Other than the kitchen, the downstairs rooms were now used only occasionally to entertain Elizabeth's bridge club.

After a year, Gregory could still feel where the muscle spasm had hit him, but he was confident that it would not recur. He could again run four miles in twenty-six minutes, and further now he could run ten miles in seventy minutes. He did not think he could go ten miles much faster than that, but he knew he could maintain the pace longer.

At noon he dressed and showered with Fred and Gene, but he ran separately. Fred and Gene lived near one another, and ran to work each morning on various routes, all ten or twelve miles long. At noon they tried to run at racing pace. After work, they ran home, about six miles on a direct route, at about three-quarters their racing pace. They raced 10,000 and 15,000 meters, and the Marathon.

One day continuing a conversation, they ran the first lap around the park with Gregory at his pace. It always took Gregory awhile to warm up, age perhaps.

"Say," Fred said as they came around to their starting point, "let's see how you're doing."

"All right," Gregory said, although he usually liked to jog at least a mile before starting to run.

Gene sprinted ahead. Fred kept just half a pace in front of Gregory, slowly increasing the speed, pulling Gregory on. They said nothing to one another. Gregory concentrated on keeping up. The four laps went quickly.

"I'll be damned," Fred said as they slowed down. "That was almost six minutes a mile. You're doing ok, old fellow."

"Damned good," Gene said, coming around. "I'm impressed."

Fred ran on with Gene, and Gregory picked up to six-and-a-half minutes. However, he soon dropped down to a seven-minute pace. He was still glowing when they congratulated him again at the end of the run.

Johanson knew that Gregory ran at noontime because there had been joking—and some warnings from back-pain sufferers—in the office. As with Gregory's moustache—he was the only man in the office with hair on his face—Johanson elected to ignore Gregory's running.

One thing Gregory did do that spring was enter the Annual Twin City Memorial Day Run. He ran seven miles and placed third in his age category. There was even a trophy for that. Gregory had not told Elizabeth he was entering the race. Now he put his trophy up on the shelf of his closet.

Not only was there an annual run, the Twin Cities now had a Marathon. It was held the Fourth of July. After the Memorial Day run, Gregory conceived a desire to run the Marathon.

He would have only a month to train, and the books said one needed three months. However, the books also said that anyone who ran ninety—or at absolute minimum—seventy miles a week, could finish the twenty-six miles and 385 yards of the Marathon. Gregory had been averaging something over seventy miles a week nearly all spring. He could increase that easily to ninety or more.

On the other hand, he had never run farther than twenty miles. The books all spoke of the wall at twenty miles. Somewhere after twenty miles all the energy stored in your muscles is used up. Then you start burning your fat and even your protein. Not only is this a strain, it produces poisons for which you cannot take in enough oxygen to burn off. So your muscles ache and cramp, you get a stitch in your side, your lungs burn. You are weak and nauseated. When horses reach this point, they refuse to run farther. If they are beaten and are made to run farther, they can be run to death. When a human runner hits the wall, he need not stop. He can force himself on by sheer power of will.

Gregory read of the pain of the last six miles. But he also read of the joy of finishing, and of how many men older than he was had completed many Marathons, and loved the challenge.

A Marathon knocks one out. Gregory had only a month to prepare, and it would be foolish for him to run the full distance in training.

He made out a schedule. At least fifteen miles in one long slow run on Wednesdays, and up to twenty miles on Sundays. On other days he would run at least ten miles. Over the noon hour he would run for pace.

Gregory sent in his application.

The days of June flew.

Gregory had not wanted to tell Elizabeth, but he had to because she had other plans for the Fourth of July.

It was after dinner. Elizabeth sat looking at Gregory speculatively, her head cocked and one eye partially closed as she blew smoke up to the ceiling.

"I might have guessed," she said.

Gregory knew that his best mode of argument was to say as little as possible.

"I read in the paper that you got a trophy Memorial Day," Elizabeth said, her tone a curious mixture of pride and derision.

Suddenly she laughed, and Gregory knew it was all right.

"Where'd you hide it?" Elizabeth asked. "Or is it on your desk at the office?" the derision returning to her voice.

"In my closet . . ."

"Well, you might show it to me sometime," Elizabeth said, losing interest. "Go ahead. I'll make some excuse for you at the picnic. God knows I don't enjoy them much myself anymore, but the bridge club wanted to have one." She pushed herself up from the table. "Go on," she said. "Good night."

"Good night," Gregory said.

At the top of the stairs, Elizabeth turned and put her hand on Gregory's cheek. "Greggie, you be careful," she said. Then she went into her room, having forgotten all about it, Gregory was sure, by the time she had turned on the television.

Gregory had forgotten Elizabeth by the time his dinner had settled and he began his evening exercise routine.

There were several hundred runners gathered to try the Twin Cities Marathon. The attempt to order them according to best times broke down after the first row in which some top class Marathoners were seeded. Gregory was now experienced enough to understand the advantage of being up front, so he resisted elbows and shoves to maintain his place behind the front row.

Fred and Gene were there, too, but they barely nodded at him, unseeing.

Gregory did not hear the gun, but long before he was ready he was running with the crowd. Much too fast. He knew he should not be starting out so fast, but the others carried him along. At the five mile point the runners had thinned out and Gregory slowed his pace to the seven minutes a mile he had planned.

He maintained it to the ten mile marker, and then to the fifteen. He was beginning to feel the strain, and his pace dropped to seven and a half. About a mile from the twenty-mile marker, he glanced at his watch to see that he had dropped to even slower, so he strained to make the twenty miles in two hours and twenty minutes.

Now he would see. He felt ok, but his pace had dropped to eight minutes.

Where was the wall?

There were other runners far ahead. One of them had probably won the race by now.

Gregory tried to keep his pace, but by the twenty-third mile it had dropped to nine minutes.

Then it hit him. It was not so much a wall. It was just that all the strength had drained out of him.

Gregory gasped and almost stopped, but he went on. He did not look at his watch now.

Three more miles.

On.

After time that seemed palpable, a mass to move through, there was only one more mile—and 385 yards. But Gregory had to stop.

He bent over to retch, but even in that position he felt himself moving slowly on. He walked, stopped, jogged, walked. It took him fifteen minutes to go that mile.

Then the muscles of his legs locked. He stood for a minute. For two minutes.

Suddenly there were two maniacs beside him, screaming.

"Go on, go on!" Gene yelled.

Fred said, "You can do it, go on."

Gregory shook his head. But he started up. After fifty yards he stopped.

"You've got to!" Gene yelled.

Fred spoke calmly. "Look, Greg," he said, "you've got a chance to break three-thirty." He looked at his watch. "You've got a little under four minutes, say three minutes. You can run 300 yards in three minutes. You *can*. Now come on. I'm going to pace you."

Fred started on ahead. "Come *on!*" he commanded.

Gregory started jogging. He could see nothing but Fred's feet. He felt—nothing, really. The pain was not his. It was too unbelievable to be real. Gregory ran on nothing.

He realized he had passed the finish line when he heard Gene cheering.

"Try to keep walking," Fred kept an official from taking Gregory by the arm. Gene accepted Gregory's time ticket.

"You did it," Fred said. "Three hours, twenty-nine minutes, twelve seconds. A piece of cake."

Gregory was very slow to recover. He allowed Fred and Gene to fuss over him.

"How old did you say you were?" Gene asked.

"Forty-nine."

Gene looked at Fred. "Next year he'll be in the over-fifty's. How much do you think he can improve if he trains?"

"How'd you guys do?" Gregory asked later over a beer.

"Shit," Gene said.

"We did ok," Fred said.

"They bring in those foreigners," Gene said with disgust.

"It's an open race," Fred said.

"Yeah. Say, Greg, why don't you join the Twin City Track Club?"

Gregory was reluctant, but when he found that it involved nothing more than stating the affiliation whenever he raced, he accepted Gene's invitation.

But he was not sure he would run another Marathon.

The next day he could barely run the two miles around the lake. It was a month before he began to feel right, and three months before he began to wonder if he could do better next time.

Gene had been right. There were not many runners over fifty in the Twin City Marathon that next year, and the longer training period helped. There was a guy from California who won the division in well under three hours, but Gregory came in second at three hours and seventeen minutes. Fred had coached him on pacing, and although he had hit the wall this time, too, it had not laid him out. Actually, Gregory had held back. Fred congratulated him, but obviously was disappointed that he had not done better.

Gregory showed this trophy to Elizabeth. She snorted, laughed, then snorted again.

"I don't really know what to make of it," Elizabeth said, looking up at Gregory. "I truthfully don't know what to make of it." She set the trophy down on the table. "What's for dinner?"

Later Gregory put the trophy on top of his bookcase. Then he went to his closet and got his other trophy—Elizabeth had never followed up on her expression of interest in seeing it—and set it out on the bookcase, too.

One bright winter day on the noon-hour run, Gene said, "Hey, man, you've got to go to Boston with us."

Gregory had not decided yet whether he was going to run another Marathon. He had read in the *TCTC News* that they were trying to get enough members to go to charter a plane. Someone from the club usually went to Boston every year, but this year they wanted everyone who could qualify to race, and they wanted others to go along to fill up the charter.

"Qualifying is only 3:30, and you've broken that," Gene said.

"We'd like you to come," Fred added.

Gregory mulled it over for several weeks, but the decision had been made the moment Gene had mentioned Boston.

Still, it was a bit frightening. There were those hills, and the heat. The running in Minnesota was mostly flat, and mostly cool. Gregory trained, but he did fear Boston.

Then three days before they were to leave, Elizabeth came down with the flu. The next day the doctor said it might be pneumonia, and she was for no reason to get out of bed.

Gregory felt relieved. He wanted to go to Boston, yet he grasped eagerly this straw of an excuse. He spoke seriously with concern in his voice to Fred on the phone, but it echoed back hollow. Gregory purposefully put aside his desire to run the Boston Marathon. For Elizabeth. He felt empty.

On the day of the race, Elizabeth had a fever. She was up the next day, however.

Gregory read in the paper how the Track Club members had done. He did not know many of them. Fred and Gene had good times, but were nowhere near the top.

Too bad.

Gregory was in the doldrums all summer. Why had he not gone to Boston? He was getting old. But men in their seventies ran it.

Summer came again and Gregory ran his third Twin Cities Marathon. Again he preserved himself, ran it ten minutes slower than the year before, felt fine afterward, and did not place.

Gregory ran, but he stopped pushing. One cold noon in early winter, Gene said, "You seem bogged down."

"I know it," Gregory said. "I enjoy running a lot, but I don't know . . ."

"You'd have liked Boston," Fred said.

Fred had said this to Gregory before, but this time it hit a different chord. It was true. Gregory would have liked Boston. The thought invigorated him. He would like Boston.

The next day Gregory asked, "Is the Club going to Boston in the spring?"

"No," Fred said, "not as a group. Some of us were thinking about it. You interested?"

"Yes," Gregory said. "I want to go." After a moment he added, "And this time I will."

"Well, Jesus," Gene said to Fred, "let's not think about it any more and just go."

"All right," Fred replied slowly. "Sure, let's go. And we've got all winter," he said. "Greg, I think you can break three. Actually, I think you could do even better than that."

Gregory began to push again.

They flew to Boston a week early to get acclimatized, and to practice on the hills. There were seven Twin City runners. Only Fred and Gene had run the Boston before.

"I sure don't like these hills," Gene said on one of their practice runs.

"Yes, we know," Fred replied. "I believe you've said that before."

"Right you are. I sure don't like these hills."

The hills were hurting Gregory, too. His ankles were not used to the angles, and his knees were sore from the shock of pounding downhill. At least the weather was cool.

They stayed in a small hotel near Harvard Square, Gene's choice. It had been many years since Gregory had been out for any length of time with the boys, since he was married, he guessed. He was twenty-two years older than the oldest of the other six, but the nature of their mutual enterprise—and his time which ranked him right in the middle of them—made them treat him mostly as they treated one another. They joked about fixing him up with a Radcliffe girl.

Out with the boys, but incredibly wholesome. They ate in different restaurants in the pleasant neighborhood, loading on plenty of carbohydrates in a pancake house the last three days before the race. Gregory felt good, in good health. He wondered how many men nearly fifty-five felt as good as he did.

The day of the race dawned hazy and still. It was going to be a scorcher. Bad luck.

There were several thousand runners and the crush of the lineup was claustrophobic. As always, it started too soon, but Gregory was so far back that it was two minutes before his part of the mob got moving. Then it was too fast on the downhill course at the beginning.

As soon as he could, Gregory set himself on a seven-minute pace. He wanted to better his best time if possible, but the first thing was to finish, survival.

Some of the paved streets were rough, and often the crowd pressed too close. More than a million spectators were predicted. They made Gregory nervous, although for the most part their yelling was friendly.

The day was getting warmer. It was a muggy heat. Gregory yearned for a breeze. He could not keep his pace.

When the bad hills began, Gregory lost all consciousness of anything else. All he knew was that his strength was going. He passed twenty miles and started up the longest hill, Heartbreak Hill.

It was the heat and the humidity. Gregory went slower and slower. Halfway up he stopped.

"Go on, go on," someone yelled. "Over the top is out."

Gregory struggled on. At least he would get to the top of Heartbreak Hill. He walked ten yards, then jogged very slowly on to the top.

There someone sprayed him with a hose. He had not expected the shock. Someone else handed him a cup. He took a sip and choked. It was extremely sweet limeade. He dropped the cup and looked around.

"All downhill from here," someone said. The man put his arm around Gregory's shoulders, urged him on, and slapped him on the bottom as he started to run again.

Gregory knew it was not all downhill from here.

At about twenty-three miles he was done again. But the crowd would not let him stop. Or, he did not want to stop, and the crowd spoke his desire out loud. He jogged and walked. He stopped bent over, and then staggered on.

Sooner than he had expected he crossed the finish line. He did **not want to know his time, but he could not avoid seeing it. Odd,** it had not seemed that long, but it had taken him nearly four

122

hours. Almost thirty minutes longer than any of his previous Marathons. Another minute and he would not even have broken four hours.

Yet, he felt a surge of joy. By God, he had done it, he had finished the Boston Marathon.

The whole scene was chaotic, and Gregory made no effort to locate any of the other Track Club members. Someone gave him a ride back to the hotel, where he showered and changed. Then he went to the pub where they had agreed to meet.

Five of the others were there. Two of them were slower than Gregory, and for a moment his mood was deflated. Then he realized that they had dropped out. Their slowest runner was not there, and Gregory thought he would probably plod on until he finished.

"Slow, eh?" Fred stated. The table had several pitchers and many glasses on it. Fred peered into a glass, then filled it with foaming beer for Gregory. Gregory took it automatically.

"How'd you do?"

"Slow," Fred said.

Gregory looked at Gene, who did not look up.

Fred looked from Gene to Gregory. "Gene dropped out in the hills."

"Too hot," Gene said firmly, glaring at Gregory. "I could have gone on, but I wasn't getting anywhere. I decided it would be crazy to kill myself in that heat just to finish."

Gregory's glass was halfway to his mouth, and his mouth was open. He sat like that, looking at Gene. Gene took a long drink of beer.

It had never occurred to Gregory to quit. Just because his time was shot. The point, he thought, was to finish. He was so set on finishing that only now was he beginning to realize how bad he felt.

Gregory set the glass carefully back down on the table, started to get up, then turned on his chair and retched and retched and retched.

12

When Gregory returned from Boston, Elizabeth was gone. There was a note on the kitchen table. It was dated the day after Gregory had left for Boston.

Dear Greggie

Mama called this morning to say that Daddy died yesterday of a heart attack. I'm going to Florida now. I've mislaid the name of your hotel, and I know you wouldn't want to leave anyway. I mean, I know I could find out somehow where you're staying, but it doesn't matter. I doubt if Mama will know the difference. Anyway, I'm going. I'll probably stay awhile with Mama, so call me when you get back.

Love
Liz

Gregory read the note a second time. The funeral was over by now. And it was just like Elizabeth to mislay the address. If she did. It was kind of her to let him go. And she knew that he would not feel much. He had never been close to her parents.

He thought of his own parents, still going strong in Northwood. He seldom thought of them. The old man was, what?, seventy-seven now, and he still went to the office of his one-man insurance agency on main street every day. Gregory's mother wrote regularly, once a month, letters full of gossip about people Gregory barely remembered, about old classmates of his, and about people his mother seemed to think he knew, although he recognized the names only from their recurrence in the letters. Gregory supposed his parents would live another ten years at least.

Gregory glanced at the kitchen clock and decided to wait until five to call Elizabeth, after the prices changed.

Toward the end of their conversation, Elizabeth said, "Greggie, I think I'm going to have to stay awhile longer. Mama is really not in very good shape, and someone will have to take care of her awhile. There's nothing much to do there around the house, so I might as well stay and take care of her myself. What do you think? You can get along all right alone, can't you? You don't care, do you? It would be one less to cook for." She started to laugh, but cut it off. "I mean, Greggie, you'll get along ok, won't you? Mama isn't so good."

Gregory knew that Elizabeth's mother was senile. Elizabeth's father had, in fact, been taking care of the old woman. But he died first.

"No, I don't mind," Gregory said. "Take as long as you need."

Neither of them mentioned Boston.

Gregory hung up the phone and started to prepare dinner. Afterward he went upstairs and read while his meal settled. Then he changed into a sweat suit and stood on his mat. Just before he had left for Boston he had purchased a copy of a book titled *The Complete Illustrated Book of Yoga*, which he had read on the plane. Now he started in on the first course.

It ought to be just the thing for his aching bones and muscles.

13

The summer passed, Thanksgiving came and went. Gregory stayed in Minneapolis Elizabeth stayed in Florida. In years past the twins had returned home to Minneapolis for Christmas, but this year Elizabeth had arranged for them all to have Christmas in Florida. "Mama can't travel," she wrote.

It was the first time Gregory had seen Elizabeth since just before Boston. She did not seem changed. The twins and their spouses, though, seemed too adult. Gregory recognized his younger self in Donald, and Elizabeth's in Constance. The grandchildren were much more interested in television and the beach than in their grandfather. Gregory had to admit that he was not much interested in them, either. He could never imagine what was in their minds. He supposed they thought him crazy for running. Donald asked him if he could be overdoing it. Gregory smiled and shook his head.

Gregory stayed in the big rambling house for a week after the twins and their families had left. Elizabeth's father had bought it nearly thirty years before, with investment and retirement in mind. It had been a good buy, appreciating in value many times over. It had been kept up well. Beach houses are not made that big and that solid anymore.

"I sure don't miss that Minnesota winter," Elizabeth said.

Gregory left after New Year's. When he got back to Minneapolis, he boxed up and mailed the rest of Elizabeth's lightweight clothes and various other things she had asked for. He put all her winter clothes in plastic bags, pulled the venetian blinds shut, took one last look around the old bedroom, and closed the door.

The next five years Gregory saw Elizabeth only at Christmas, and for that matter, the twins' families only then, too. Donald sometimes stopped through Minneapolis for a few hours on business, and took Gregory out to dinner. Donald never had time to come out to the house. None of them referred to the situation as a separation.

The year Gregory was sixty, the *Minneapolis Tribune* featured him in their article on the Annual Twin City Marathon. Gregory had not returned to Boston, but he continued to run every day. More than before, for he had started getting up earlier in the morning, and (as he was quoted in the paper) what was there to do then but run? His times had not diminished, but his endurance had increased. Several times he had run thirty miles—slowly—just because he felt like it. He could probably run fifty, he told the reporter. He just had not felt like it yet. And each year he found that he had the desire to run the Twin City Marathon.

Gregory's work at the office had increased over the years. He had not been made vice-president, but he was Johanson's chief confidant and consultant, and he knew the business inside out. Even after thirty-four years, Gregory found the work interesting.

"Say, I saw that piece about you in the paper." Johanson said. "Pretty good for an old man, eh?" Ever since people in the office had congratulated Gregory on finishing the Boston Marathon—such is its fame—Johanson had taken a perfunctory interest in Gregory's running.

"Come on in, I want to ask you something," Johanson said now.

Gregory could tell that Johanson was not at all feeling jovial.

"Drink?" Johanson asked. Johanson had started drinking openly in front of Gregory only in the last five years.

Gregory shook his head. Johanson weighed the bottle, then put it back in the drawer without opening it.

"Greg," Johanson said, "I'm five years older than you."

Gregory knew that.

"They want me to retire," Johanson said abruptly. "I'm sixty-five, and they say I ought to retire. Go fishing!" he said with great scorn. Deliberately he opened the drawer, took out the bottle and a water glass, and poured the glass half full of rye whiskey. He put the bottle back and let the glass sit untouched on the desk before him, staring over it at Gregory.

Gregory cleared his throat.

"Say it," Johanson said, taking a sip of the whiskey.

"I don't see why," Gregory said, "you should retire."

"Not this," Johanson said, saluting Gregory with the glass and taking another sip.

Gregory grinned. "Certainly not that, Joe. You know you could hold a quart and nobody'd know the difference."

Johanson permitted himself a brief smile.

"Greg," he went on, "they're serious. They really do want me to retire. Out. What would I do?"

But Gregory's thoughts had taken a tangent.

"Joe," he said, "that was a very good retirement plan we worked out when I first came to work here, wasn't it?"

Johanson sighed. "Yes, yes, it's a good plan."

"I haven't looked at it for years," Gregory said, "but it has, I recall, a provision for early retirement at three-quarters or some-such, with full pickup later, doesn't it?"

Johanson looked grim. "I've had occasion to look at it carefully recently," he said with a touch of irony. "Yes, it has provision for early retirement. I forget the percentages, but it goes up as you get older. You have to take that percentage until you're seventy, then it picks up at what it would have been if you'd retired at sixty-five. Why?" Johanson asked, unamused. "Are you thinking of retiring early?"

Gregory had forgotten Johanson's problem. "Yes, Joe, I am. I'll be sixty-one in September, and I want to retire the day after my birthday. I'll write you a formal request and resignation." Gregory stood up.

Johanson downed the remaining half of his whiskey at a gulp and held the empty glass up, looking at it. "Boy, that does it," he said. His voice rose. "That's it, old buddy, that'll be the end. If *you* retire . . . And what'll you do? Go somewhere and run around in those pansy pants?"

Gregory's forehead contorted and he smiled weakly. He had always liked Johanson. There was nothing he could say. He let himself out of the office.

That is what he would do. He would go someplace and run. Like that time in Colorado. He had run a few times outside Minneapolis, around lakes and in state parks. Now he would go see a few places he had read about, and yes, he would run.

The excitement of it did not hit Gregory until that night. He had never thought about retiring early, but it had come to him as he was sitting there in Johanson's office as though he had planned it for years.

He would have plenty of money. He did not need much. Elizabeth's father had invested well and she had not asked for a penny, her mother had plenty. The twins needed none. He would get social security in four more years. In fact, he would be rich.

Gregory's thoughts kept him from sleeping most of the night. The next day he wrote a formal letter to Johanson, resigning and asking for early retirement. He told no one else in the office, and Johanson did not argue. He took the letter and seemed prepared to weather the storm.

Gregory busied himself with getting ready. Should he rent the house? No, not at first. He did not need to. He looked in the basement for camping gear. Donald had taken most of it, and the old family tent had rotted out. Gregory toyed with the notion of getting a Volkswagen camper. He went to an agency, but he did not like the salesman. The camper seemed all right, but it was so expensive. Gregory decided to wait. He bought a new tent and some other gear.

A week passed. Johanson had said nothing about Gregory's letter. Gregory thought about writing the insurance agency about his retiring early, but he did not do it.

Just what *would* he do?

Another week passed. Gregory had prepared all he could, and it was only the middle of July. He got out some maps, but could not concentrate on them. Where should he go?

After a sleepless night, Gregory went in to see Johanson.

"Joe, ..."

"I'm glad you came in, Greg," Johanson said briskly. "I was just going to call you." Johanson was his old self. "I've had to make some changes around here. That fellow you call Buster Brown, well," Johanson smiled fiercely for a moment, "he's decided to move on to a larger firm, someplace where there's more room for him to maneuver. That leaves a vice-presidency open." Johanson raised his voice slightly and talked fully to leave no spaces for interruption. "So we've made you a vice-president, and it was high time, too. Now," he went on without pause, "I know you want a vacation, and you deserve a good one. I've already shifted your payroll to the percentage shares plan, and that goes on twelve months a year, year in, year out. And that means you can take a long vacation with full pay, anytime. Take a month, Greg, take six weeks if you want. Come back the first of September, and we'll show them."

Johanson looked directly at Gregory for the first time. "Congratulations," he said, holding out that awkward shovel of a hand.

Gregory looked at the beads of sweat on Johanson's brow. They were the only sign of his yearning. Johanson's hand was as steady as a rock.

Gregory paused only a moment, then he shook Johanson's hand. The last time he had been in Johanson's office he had thought he wanted to retire early. That seemed to have been a kind of fit of temporary madness. Now Gregory was immensely pleased at having been made a vice-president. Never mind how it had come about (and if Johanson thought Gregory had been exerting pressure, he would like him the better for it), Gregory had always felt that he deserved it, and had resented not getting it. His pleasure and the flood of gratitude he felt now showed him how unsuccessful he had been in holding down that desire and resentment.

"I . . . , thank you, Joe," Gregory said. "And . . . yes, I would like to take a vacation. Why don't I stay on now until the end of July? I'll take August off."

Fine, fine," Johanson beamed. "Well, this calls for a celebration. But I confess that I hadn't planned it for this morning. I hope you can wait until four o'clock?"

Gregory felt so pleased that during the noon run he told Fred about it. Gene had moved on, and now Fred always ran at Gregory's pace. Gregory suspected that Fred was glad enough to slow down.

"That's what notoriety in the papers will get you," Fred said.

At four o'clock, Johanson called the staff together and made the announcement. A caterer had brought in drinks and small open sandwiches. Everyone shook Gregory's hand, and attacked the liquor and food eagerly.

"A real happy hour," Johanson said. He was fully in command again.

Gregory attended his first board meeting the next week, and on the first of August he set out for Colorado. Donald had invited him out to go camping for a week. Then Gregory would think of something else to do.

It was not exactly camping. Donald had lived in Denver since he graduated from college, and he had purchased a condominium apartment in Winter Park for skiing. This is where they went now. Only Donald's wife and youngest son was with them. He had just graduated from high school that spring, and spent his time at the pool or roaring around in Donald's car.

"Where's he going to college?" Gregory had asked.

"He's not going right away," Donald's wife had answered. "He's going to take a year off first."

"Yeah, I know," Donald sighed in answer to Gregory's questioning glance. "He wants to find himself." Frankly, I think he's more interested in finding girls and having a good time." Donald patted his wife on the shoulder. "But by the time you've had four of them, you learn to take what comes, eh, darling?"

"He's not a bad boy," Donald's wife said.

"Say, why don't we take an overnight backpack trip?" Gregory asked on another day.

"Not me," his grandson replied. "Got a date."

"Donald?"

"No, I'm not much for that anymore."

"Remember that time the summer before you started to college?" Gregory asked.

"Do I? What a time!"

"And Long's Peak?"

"We were crazy," Donald said. "Just plain crazy. It was a wonder we weren't killed. And that fall you took. I was scared, but I thought I could hold you. It was a wonder you weren't killed."

Gregory wished he had not brought it up. His memories were obviously fonder than Donald's.

The day before they were to return to Denver, Gregory saw Donald standing at the window, watching him as he returned from his run. Gregory sighed. This was too predictable.

"Dad . . ."

"You think I'll hurt myself running, don't you? Drop over dead."

"Well, I've heard that it's good protection from heart attacks. But you'll be sixty-one next month."

"Don't worry, Donald. I'll take care of myself. Really I will." Gregory lay a hand on Donald's arm. "What have you heard from your mother?" It was the first time they had mentioned Elizabeth.

"Not much. Much the same as you, I suppose."

Maybe I'll drive down to see her after I leave here," Gregory said. There was nothing much else he wanted to do. He had never been to the west coast. So, well, maybe he would never go to the west coast. He had not lost anything out there.

Gregory drove without haste. He stopped wherever he saw a place that looked interesting for running and exploring. He camped out, sometimes in campgrounds where there were showers, but as often in out-of-the-way places on side roads. He was used to being alone, and he enjoyed the changes of scenery. But he wondered why he had thought of such travel as any sort of life that he would retire early to live.

Elizabeth was glad to see him, but paid little attention to him. She complained of the summer Florida heat. Gregory did not care for her cooking now, and pleased her by taking her out to dinner four of the five days he stayed in her mother's house.

Elizabeth's mother was almost totally helpless. Elizabeth tended her briskly. It unnerved Gregory that Elizabeth would often just let her mother whimper and that she went off when she pleased to play bridge, or to dinner. Elizabeth assured Gregory that it was perfectly all right.

"Mama's not going anywhere."

Gregory drove up through the Ozarks and the midwest to Minneapolis. He stopped overnight in Northwood. Two years before, to Gregory's surprise, his father had died. He had had cancer of the lower colon, for years, evidently, and by the time he told anyone of his problem, it was too late. Gregory shed tears at the funeral. He remembered many things about his father that he had not thought of for years, and he felt a general sense of emptiness and loss.

Gregory's mother still lived in the house he had grown up in. She had not changed much for twenty years that he could tell, even though she was now eighty years old. Gregory's sister had married the banker's son—now the banker—a man who from childhood Gregory had never been able to tolerate. But they lived in Northwood and looked after his mother, for which Gregory was grateful.

Gregory had sent his mother a clipping of the article in the *Minneapolis Tribune* about his running. She had it pinned on the kitchen wall, with many other clippings and pictures of her children, grandchildren, and great grandchildren. She complimented Gregory on how fit he looked, looking meaningfully across the dinner table at Gregory's brother-in-law, who was a slob and was eating like a pig.

"Now Mama," the banker grinned with his mouth full.

Gregory arrived in Minneapolis four days before he was due. He called Johanson to ask if it would be all right to take the rest of the month. There were some things he wanted to do around the house. Gregory knew Johanson would agree, he just wanted him to know that he was back.

Gregory's bedroom was pleasant, but he had lately thought it too small. He wanted room for more bookcases, and also he was tired of living on two floors. He liked living upstairs, particularly because the room faced southwest over the lake.

He had often thought of removing the partition between his room and Constance's old room. He had determined that the wall was bearing no weight, or not enough to matter. Now he took everything in Constance's room to the basement, then smashed out the wall, opening a room the length of the house.

He had been going to do all the work himself, but after clearing up the debris, he called in a carpenter to patch up. The carpenter also built in the bookcases Gregory wanted, and put in cabinets and counters in the far corner of the room where Gregory was having a kitchen sink, a small stove, and a refrigerator installed.

"You could have a real nice breakfast nook built in that front corner, so you could eat looking over the lake," the carpenter suggested.

"All right," Gregory agreed.

Two weeks after he returned to work, Gregory's new apartment was ready. He now had more room for his exercise mat—on which he still slept—and the apartment was quite spacious. He arranged his books—mysteries, mountain climbing, small boat sailors, health and physical fitness—in one section of the new shelves, and those on running and his back copies of *Runner's World* in another. He had had a niche made for his two trophies—he did not expect to win any more, although perhaps if he ran the Twin City Marathon for another ten years he could win the over-seventy division for lack of competitors.

He was especially pleased with the view over the lake, and after a month asked the carpenter to return to install a wide picture window in the center of the wall where the old partition had joined. There were windows on either side wall, as well, looking out on big trees that shielded Gregory's house from his neighbors.

Gregory disconnected the downstairs appliances. He left the downstairs radiators open only enough to allow circulation so they would not freeze. He had a heating man come to change the thermostat from the front room to his apartment. When winter came, he was ready.

14

One day during a small crisis at work, Johanson dropped dead on the floor. He was sixty-seven years old. Gregory had been in his own office, but he had heard Johanson fall, the hush, and then the babble. While someone called a doctor, Gregory bent down and put his fingers on Johanson's neck. There was no pulse at all. Gregory pressed sharply with the heel of his hand on Johanson's chest. Then—although Johanson was surely dead—Gregory tried ten minutes of mouth-to-mouth resuscitation.

Johanson's mouth had the sweet taste of a drinker.

He had had a massive coronary attack.

Johanson had never married. Two brothers, one older and one younger, came to the funeral. Johanson had left several hundred thousand dollars to be shared equally between them. He left his shares of the business—a clear majority—to Gregory. When this became known, the other vice-presidents elected Gregory president of the company. It pleased him considerably less than his promotion to vice-president had. However, he moved into Johanson's old office and changed little for a smooth transition.

This time Gregory thought it over for six months. He was sixty-two, and he decided that he would definitely retire when he was sixty-five. He waited another six months, then called the man he always thought of as Buster Brown. Brown listened to Gregory on the phone, visited the office several days in a row, and a month later rejoined the firm as senior vice-president. Gregory thought Brown had matured considerably, and progressively turned all of the executive duties over to him. When Gregory retired, Brown had virtually been running the firm for the last six months. Gregory gave him proxy on his shares of the business, with option to buy them on any schedule Brown could afford.

Gregory had worked there for forty-one years. He had enjoyed his work, had risen to the top, and had successfully guided the firm during the last three years. He shook everyone's hand when he left, accepted their gifts of a plaque and an inscribed gold watch. He set the plaque in the niche behind his two running trophies, and lay the watch between them. He never visited the office again.

Gregory had had some trouble with constipation when he was younger, but this had cleared up in his mid-forties after he had started eating bran and fresh vegetables—and avoiding sugar and processed flour—as advised in the health literature that he still read occasionally. The only physical examinations he had had for twenty years were superficial check-ups before the Marathons he had run. He had not had a cold nor the flu nor any sickness for a dozen years. Whether this was because he took five grams of vitamin C a day he did not know. He had not had many colds before he began that, either.

Now he decided—in retirement—that he ought to have a thorough physical. He checked in at the university medical clinic for a three-day examination.

Immediately he ran into trouble. The doctor supervising his examination was alarmed at Gregory's low blood pressure, his slow pulse, and his odd EKG. He ordered the EKG repeated, and he made fluoroscope photographs of Gregory's heart. The EKG showed the same unusual pattern as before, and Gregory' heart was a third larger than was normal for a man his size and age.

Gregory knew all about this from having read articles in *Run-*

ner's World. It was perfectly normal—for a runner. But when Gregory tried to explain this, the doctor was alarmed that Gregory did so much running, and he spoke ominously about the dangers of an enlarged athlete's heart.

Gregory knew that this view was completely outdated and discredited, but he also knew that some runners had been refused permission to race by doctors who still abided by the old prejudices.

The tests proceeded. Gregory had no trace of cancer in his colon, nor any other abnormality, except that for his age he was in superb health.

"Except for this heart problem," the doctor said severely during his final counseling.

"I don't have a heart problem," Gregory said.

The doctor started in, but Gregory cut him off. "Look doctor, aren't there any doctors in this clinic who are runners?"

"I don't see what that would prove," the doctor said.

The nurse then leaned over and whispered in the doctor's ear.

"All right," he said, "see if you can find him. One of the interns," he went on to Gregory, "is a runner." He continued to summarize the rest of the test results.

"Hey, good to see you," the intern said. "You look in great shape. No problems, I hope?"

Gregory recognized the intern as a Track Club member, but he did not know his name.

Gregory started to explain, but the doctor silenced him, and then showed the intern Gregory's pulse chart, his EKGs, and the photographs of his enlarged heart.

The intern glanced at Gregory, then explained in medical terminology how it happened that Gregory had these irregularities. "He's not abnormal," the intern concluded. "We're just not used to seeing many really healthy specimens."

The doctor looked dubious, but he had given in. "I think he might put on a little more weight," he said.

Gregory had not checked his weight for years, and was surprised himself to find that he weighed only 131.

The intern winked at Gregory. "He'll outlive us all," he said. He shook Gregory's hand. "Sure good to meet you, finally. I hope my tests look like that when I'm your age." As he walked out the door he said, "Hang in there."

At your age," the doctor concluded, "you should have a thorough physical examination once a year."

Gregory doubted that he would.

Gregory began to spend several hours every day at the Twin City Track Club. They had rooms and a fine library in the Athletic Club building. Gregory worked out in the weight room, and on bad days he ran on the indoor track. He also swam laps to keep limber, although he found swimming back and forth in the pool a terrible bore. On good days he often ran the five miles to the building, but as often he rode Donald's old ten-speed bicycle that he had found and fixed up that time he was looking for camping gear. In very bad snowy weather, he walked. He tried to drive his car as seldom as possible, partly because of the energy crisis, but mostly because when he drove he sometimes automatically arrived at his old office building, and this gave him no pleasure.

In his seventieth year, Gregory won another trophy in the Twin City Marathon. Second place in the over-seventy division. The winner was one of those foreigners, a retired doctor from California who drove a motorized house van the size of a small truck. It was painted in psychodelic colors on both sides around a message in stylized lettering that said: 73 AND STILL RUNNING. This septenarian runner moved from race to race, making quite a show of himself. Gregory had dinner with him in his house van.

"It will soon be time to paint out that '73' and paint in '74'," Doc said. "It really makes me look forward to birthdays."

"It must be quite a thrill," Gregory said dryly.

It was too flamboyant for Gregory, but he enjoyed the talk and the health food dinner.

There was just room in the niche—with squeezing—for Gregory's third trophy. He decided that he would not enter the Marathon next year. He would be one of the officials. For several years he had been helping at the Track Club meets. He also worked on the Club books, and arranged flights. He had been tempted to go along on one of the charters to Boston, but he preferred to keep his memory of the one time intact.

The twins' children were grown, and Gregory had not seen Elizabeth for several years. Then one evening she called.

"Mama died a few months ago," she said.

"Oh, I'm sorry."

"No matter. God, she hung on a long time. Anyway, I'm sort of tired of it here. I'm beginning to miss the seasons, even snow, and I thought I might come home."

Gregory said nothing.

"Greggie? Greggie, you don't mind, do you?"

"No," Gregory said slowly. "All right. When will you come?"

"Oh, I don't know. Not for a while. I thought of selling the old place here, but the income tax would take so much of it. I can get a whopping rent for it, so I'm seeing about turning it over to a rental agency who'll handle it for me. I'll let you know."

"All right."

"Greggie . . . thanks."

"It's all right, Elizabeth." Gregory said. "I'll look forward to seeing you."

They hung up.

Gregory sat in the kitchen downstairs where he had left the phone. He had disconnected the one in Elizabeth's bedroom years ago. Anyone who wanted to talk to him on the phone had to desire to badly enough to let it ring ten or fifteen times, to give Gregory time to hear it and to get downstairs.

He lay awake on his mat that night thinking. After his run the next morning, he called the carpenter and the plumber, who arrived that afternoon on his pleas of urgency. By then he had cleared out the family room that opened off the kitchen. It was large and well-lighted, but not entirely weatherproof. Now Gregory had new double-track storm windows installed. He had the partition concealing a toilet stool and sink torn out, and a new wall built to enclose a full bathroom with tiled floor and over-sized tub. He had railings installed to grip when getting in and out of the tub. There was a large closet, but it had shelves. Gregory had these torn out and clothes racks installed. In the main room he had wall-to-wall carpeting put down. This all took ten days of frantic work, during which time Gregory reattached and tested all the appliances in the kitchen. He opened and aired the living room and dining room, and had the thermostat reinstalled downstairs. There would be no problem with heat upstairs with Elizabeth controlling the thermostat downstairs.

Then Gregory and the carpenter carried down the double bed and the other furniture from Elizabeth's old bedroom. The family room still was spacious, even with the bed. Gregory quickly asked the carpenter to help him more, and they moved Constance's old desk, easy chair, floor lamp, and bookcases up from where Gregory had stored them in the basement.

Gregory was beginning to like this downstairs apartment, even if it did face the street. He tested the color television, which still worked all right. He brought down all of Elizabeth's winter clothes and hung them in the closet. Now the master bedroom was bare. Only Gregory's things remained upstairs.

Gregory sat in the easy chair in Elizabeth's new bedroom and tried to think of what he had forgotten. He got up and went to the phone in the kitchen and arranged to have two new phones installed, one up in his apartment with the old number, and one in Elizabeth's name with a new number in the new bedroom downstairs. He asked also that the kitchen phone be changed to Elizabeth's name and number.

Their mail would come to the same address. The utilities would remain in his name. He guessed that was it.

Elizabeth did not call again, but one afternoon he came home and immediately smelled that she had arrived. He fingered the ash tray on the kitchen table and glanced into the room he had prepared. He was relieved to see an open suitcase on the bed. Already the room had taken on the slight disarray that bespoke Elizabeth. It sounded as though she were in the bath tub.

Gregory sprinted up the stairs two at a time. Elizabeth had been up here, but nothing had been touched. Well, maybe the gold watch had been moved slightly.

Gregory sat down and then remembered that there had been no evening paper on the lawn. He would have to subscribe to the morning paper again for Elizabeth. He was too agitated to read now, anyway. He paced the room, and then began a yoga routine on the mat. An hour later he went back downstairs.

"Oh, Greggie, you gave me a start," Elizabeth said.

Gregory went forward to be hugged.

"Skin and bones," Elizabeth said. There was that booming laugh again.

Gregory stepped back and smiled. Elizabeth talked. She was a huge old woman now, but the same girl was there, somehow, somewhere, the one he had married so many years ago. He had not expected to be so touched.

"All these winter clothes," she laughed, indicating them spread across the bed and chairs. "Not only are they out of style, they've *shrunk*."

Gregory moved some clothes off the easy chair to sit and listen as Elizabeth moved about, settling in.

"This is nice, this room," Elizabeth said.

Gregory felt guilty. "I thought for the twin's visits . . ." he lied.

"Oh," Elizabeth said, the old sarcasm rising in her voice. "It doesn't matter." She lit a cigarette. "And don't you worry," she went on. "I went upstairs and saw your apartment. Those stairs!" Her voice relaxed. "Don't worry. I won't go up there again. Not those stairs." She walked by, stroking Gregory's cheek absently as she passed. "I won't bother you."

"What about dinner?" Gregory asked. "Shall we go out?"

"No, let's not go out. I look such a fright. Let's eat at home. But Greggie," she went on, "there's not a speck to eat in the kitchen." She laughed, "Not even salt."

Gregory gave a start. Something else he had forgotten.

"Let's go to the supermarket and get some food," Elizabeth said.

The car was stubborn, but it started. Gregory had not been to the supermarket for some years. The little shopping area half a mile from his house had deteriorated and changed in character, but along with head shops and record shops had come a pleasant health food store and a small fruit and vegetable market. Gregory did all his shopping there.

At the supermarket Elizabeth loaded three carts. The bill came to over $150. Gregory wrote a check which the manager accepted with reluctance. He said the rules were that they had to have a check-cashing ID card. Elizabeth filled out an application for one.

Another thing Gregory had forgotten was the checking account. He had never changed it from the joint account with Elizabeth, although she had not written a check on it during all the years she had spent in Florida. Gregory saw no reason to change it now. It did not matter.

At home, Elizabeth fried steak and made mashed potatoes and gravy. She now drank beer with her meals. Gregory picked at his food. He had eaten very little meat in recent years, and he had had no fried food or gravy for many years.

Elizabeth laughed and took his plate to finish it. "I guess we wont't be eating together much, will we?" she said.

Gregory refused the cream pie and went to the refrigerator to get some grapes for his desert.

"Well," Gregory said abruptly when Elizabeth had finished her coffee and cigarette. "Thanks for dinner." He got up. "Good night."

"Good night," Elizabeth said. She poured another cup of coffee.

Gregory walked upstairs to his apartment. Elizabeth was obese. She was short of breath and she smoked and drank too much. Gregory was thin. They said that no one who ran as much as he did would ever die of a heart attack. However, Gregory knew that Elizabeth would outlive him.

15

At three o'clock in the afternoon on a day in late winter, he puts down his book. He undresses and puts on wool knee socks. Over these he pulls a pair of duofold long underwear bottoms. He puts on the underwear top, and over it a turtleneck jersey. Then he does ten minutes of stretching exercises on the mat in the corner of the room. He pulls on a pair of warmup-suit pants and zips down the legs at the bottom. Then he sits down and laces on his running shoes. Standing again, he jerks his way into a crew-necked wool sweater. He shrugs on the warmup-suit jacket, zips it up, and then, wool mittens and stocking cap in hand, he goes downstairs.

As he walks through the hall, he can hear television through a closed door off the kitchen. Stepping out the front door, he pulls the wool cap over the thin white hair on his head, and puts on his mittens. Despite the brightness of the day, the air is biting, colder than he had expected. There is little heat in the afternoon sun. He does not go back for his face mask.

He waits until he is used to the air, then jogs slowly down to the lake. There is only a brushing of snow on the bare ground, and great patches of lake ice are clear. The trail around the lake is worn. He starts around.

The sun sinks lower and casts a beam of pale red onto the lake. A picture window in the middle of the second story of the house that overlooks the lake flashes brilliantly. Gregory is the small figure across the lake, running.

INTERVIEW WITH A WINNER

What was it like?
like losing
same bloody feet
blazing tendons
same sweet release
melancholia of exhaustion

What did you win?
a chance

For what?
to do it again
that wasn't it
either

What did you get?
through

What's left for you?
tomorrow's race

losing is worse

—Donald Finkel
A Mote in Heaven's Eye
New York: Atheneum, 1975